EASY *Ride*

SOUTH FLORIDA RIDERS · BOOK THREE

BREEZIE BENNETT

EASY RIDE
South Florida Riders

ISBN Print: 978-1-7341760-3-2
ISBN Ebook: 978-1-7341760-2-5

Published by Palm Island Publishing
Interior Formatting: Author E.M.S.

The South Florida Riders Series

Wild Ride
Slow Ride
Easy Ride
Thrill Ride
Rough Ride
Sweet Ride
Sleigh Ride

For a complete list, buy links, and reading order of all my books, visit https://breeziebennett.com.

Be sure to sign up for my newsletter to find out when the next book is released!

one

Chase

"I can't believe I'm about to bang Chase Kennedy. *The* Chase Kennedy."

Yeah, babe. I've heard that phrase more than a few times. "Well, aren't you forward?" I ask the smoking-hot blonde as she flops down onto my bed. I admire her top-notch set of fake tits and legs that go on for a mile.

"Forward is the only way to be when you know *exactly* what you want." She rolls over on the bed and reaches her hand out for me to join her.

My mind flashes to Leo and Elliot giving me a total dad lecture at the Atlantic earlier. *Blah, blah, blah, single life gets old... Meaningless sex is empty... You're not truly happy.*

I laugh to myself as I yank my shirt off and lie down on the bed with Megan Fox's secret twin. Sorry, Sterling and Danes, commitment might work for you guys, but this shit will never get old, and *maturity* is dumb and overrated.

"So, you said you're a model?" I ask with a nod.

"*Super*model," she corrects, staring into my eyes in a way that makes me feel like she can read me like a book. Hell, she probably can. *Player, fuckboy, Casanova*... I don't give a shit. What you see is what you get.

"Well, isn't that just...*super*?" I give her a wink and lean in for a kiss. Another night, another easy lay. Can't fucking wait for the season to start.

Right as I'm about to kiss Katie (*Kaylee? God, I'm an asshole*), my phone buzzes with a call in my pocket.

Incoming call: Nit Whit Cooper

"Shit," I say under my breath. "I gotta take this." I hop off the bed and step into the oversized living room of my twenty-third floor apartment, looking out through the floor-to-ceiling window that showcases the entire Miami Beach skyline.

"Hey, weirdo. What's up? It's so late." I hold the phone to my ear and glance at my watch, confirming that it's after two a.m.

"Troy broke up with me." The shaky, broken voice of my best friend and lifelong partner in crime makes my gut tighten.

I lean against the glass window, not sure what to say. "Shit, Whitney. Fuck. Are you sure it's for real? I mean, what was the reason?"

She sighs deeply and sniffles. "Yeah. It's over. I don't know how to feel right now. I mean...six whole years. I really thought he was the one. I don't even know. He said things were feeling...boring. I can't really say I disagree."

I pinch the bridge of my nose, wishing I could help her. She's helped me with shit probably a thousand times over the past twenty-eight years. "You know I'm no huge advocate for monogamy, but I really did think you two would make it. I'm sorry, Nit Whit."

"It's okay," she groans.

"If it helps, I always thought Troy kinda sucked. No offense."

She laughs through her tears, and the wildly familiar sound of her laughter eases the tension. "Oh, Six. What the hell am I gonna do now?"

I hear the sound of a car engine accelerating on the other end of the call. "Are you driving?" I ask her.

"Yep," she says with a sniff. "I'm gonna go back and get the rest of my shit later this week, but I just couldn't stay at our apartment. I'm going to crash at Melody's for a while."

I snort. "Your crazy hippie cousin?"

"Shut up, dickhead. She's just…unique. And more importantly, her roommate moved out, so she has the extra space."

I shake my head. "She has pink hair. Her roommate obviously knows what's up. I give you a week at that place, tops."

"Well…" Her tone shifts back to heavy and sad. "I don't really have a choice, do I?"

"You're always welcome here," I offer, thinking that having my best friend stay with me to drink Bud Lights and binge-watch *South Park* like we used to in our UF dorm room days doesn't sound so bad.

"Hah. In your high-rise Miami Beach sex house? I'll pass." I can practically hear her classic Whitney eye roll.

"Okay. Rude." I stifle a laugh.

"Come on, Chase. I'd bet my ass there's some

fake-boobed bimbo lying in your bed right now. An actress? Dancer? Model?"

I glance through the slight opening of the door to my bedroom, noticing how the thrill of tonight's particular pursuit has kinda worn off. "Damn, Nit Whit. You're good."

"Yeah, well." She sighs, and I sense yet another eye roll. "I know you better than anyone on this planet, don't I?"

"Ain't that the truth?" I look out over the scattered lights of the buildings, running a hand through my hair, wishing I could make her feel better somehow. She was my lucky charm for all of high school and college football. No matter how much I act like a douche, she just laughs and rolls her eyes. She's never been annoyed, or bothered, or even fazed by my immature antics.

"All right, I'm sorry. Get back to your sleazy model. I just needed to talk to my favorite homie for a minute." Her voice cracks a little, and I can hear her fighting more tears.

Fuck, I hate when she cries. I always have, ever since Jack Bellville pelted her in the face with a kickball at recess in fourth grade. She bawled for, like, thirty minutes, and I hated every second of it.

"Whit, come over. I'll get out some good liquor, and we can just vibe. I promise to make you laugh, if nothing else."

She's quiet for a long beat. "What about your… company?" A note of playful and sarcastic disgust registers in her voice—a tone I've become very accustomed to, although it's never stopped me from giving her the dirty details of my insane sex life. I mean, shit, she's like the ultimate bro.

"She's out the door. Promise." Sorry, Katie/Kayla/Kayleigh.

"You don't have to do that, Chase."

"I didn't have to pick up the phone either, dumbass. I got you. Now get your little self over here."

She laughs again, easing my mind. "Okay, Six. Thanks."

"Duh." I hang up the phone and quietly walk back into the bedroom. God, I hope this girl didn't fall asleep.

"There you are, sexy," she whines. "Get in this bed *now.*"

I take a long look at the dime of a chick wrapped in my black sheets—Whitney calls them my sex sheets and mocks me endlessly for them. I smile at the thought and say goodbye to the K-name supermodel.

She fumbles with a pair of heels as she hurries out of the apartment. "You're a dick, Chase."

I raise my hands defensively. "I told you, something came up with a friend. I have to be there for her."

"For *her*?" She spits the question at me as she finally gets her feet into the shoes and clicks down the hall. "You're ditching me for some other bitch?"

I hold a hand to my head, trying to understand what the fuck is even happening right now. "It's not like that. She's my—"

"Nobody turns *me* down." She flips her shiny hair over her shoulder and flings the front door open. "Fuck you, Chase Kennedy."

The door slams, and her words hang in the air. Fucking women. They make literally *zero* sense.

Except Whitney. She makes sense. But she's way more intelligent and rational than ninety percent of the smokeshows I bring back to this apartment. Which is why she's always been my best friend. And nothing more. And I fully intend to keep it that way.

Even though tonight she became single for the first time in six years.

two

Whitney

I walk down the cool, luxurious hallway of Chase's apartment building, trying to shake off the shock and hurt and flat-out confusion of getting dumped by the person I'd spent the last six solid years with.

Chase Kennedy is an unlikely best friend. If I met him now, I would probably not be able to stand him for more than three seconds. He's the world's biggest womanizer, constantly just taking his pick from a mile-long line of desperate groupies. Not to mention the douchey, cocky, hilariously obnoxious dialogue that comes out every time he opens his mouth. But…I didn't meet him now. His mom and my mom were inseparable friends and took us to a Mommy and Me group together twenty-eight years ago when we were literally in diapers.

So basically, he's been a pain in my ass since day one. But growing up with him, I've seen the Chase Kennedy his slew of fangirls will never see. I saw him fall off his bike and eat dirt at my sixth birthday party. I saw him cry his eyes out after his dog died when we were eight. I saw him puke on himself after three beers in someone's basement when we were fifteen. (And, being a true friend, I complied when he made me tell everyone at school the next day that he'd had food poisoning.)

I sat with him day after day when his mom left. Keeping him positive when he thought she might come back and helping him accept it when the divorce became final.

And…I saw him when we went to UF together, where *the* Chase Kennedy was born. His sharp football skills and that cannon of an arm brought him right into the spotlight, and he quickly realized he could have anything, and any*one*, he wanted.

But through it all, our friendship somehow never wavered. Just as his jersey number has been six since his first day of Pee Wee Football, he's been my best friend. And tonight, more than ever, I need my best friend.

"Whit," Chase says with a sympathetic laugh and open arms as he steps out of his apartment to wrap me up in a classic Kennedy hug.

I feel another wave of pain and heartbreak come over me, but being in the arms of my closest friend makes this one a little easier to bear.

I lock my hands around his back and squeeze him tightly. "Damn, boy. You've been bulking up." I pull away and teasingly pat his biceps, noticing that he's even more rock-solid and ripped than usual.

He guides me into his apartment and shuts the door. "Preseason workouts, baby." He pulls up his T-shirt and flexes a shockingly defined six-pack. "Check it out. The ladies don't stand a chance this year."

I can't help but laugh, shoving him playfully. "Did they ever *really* stand a chance?" I flop down on the soft gray sectional and look out at the picturesque nighttime view.

Chase grabs a bottle of whiskey from the kitchen cabinet and joins me on the sofa. "Here." He hands me the bottle. "Your favorite."

"No glasses or ice or anything?" I raise my brows at him. "You really never outgrew college, did you?"

"I'm trying to make you feel better, not wow you with my crystal glasses and sophisticated bullshit."

"You save that for the supermodels, I'm sure," I tease.

He shrugs. "They usually just grab me by the dick and go straight to the bedroom."

"Ew." I roll my eyes as I take a swig and relish the familiar burn as the liquor slides down my throat. "Oh, Six. You really are still that same sixteen-year-old who tried to sleep with every girl on my cheerleading squad."

He takes the bottle from me and sips, keeping his dark brown eyes locked with mine. "Except you."

I laugh softly. "Yeah, well, you knew you never had a chance."

"All through high school and college"—he runs a hand through his dirty-blond hair, a gesture he's made a million times—"everyone always thought we were hooking up. I got so much shit whenever I tried to explain to my boys that we're *literally* just friends. Without benefits."

"Hey!" I jab him in the side and take another drink. "Having me as a friend *is* the benefit."

Chase wraps his arm around me and ruffles my

already messy hair. “True that, Cooper.” He offers me the bottle again, and I accept. “So, you wanna talk about the breakup? Or is this, like, a don’t-bring-it-up sorta thing? I’m not exactly anyone’s go-to when it comes to dating and relationships.”

“Really?” I feign a gasp. “I never would have guessed.”

He gives me a half smile. “Well, it’s your call. I’m here to listen. As always.”

I lean my head on his shoulder, shutting my eyes and drawing in a slow breath. Everything about Chase has always felt like warmth and comfort and home. No matter how soulless he may appear to his infinite waitlist of one-night stands, he’s been my soft place to fall my entire life, and tonight is no different.

I wipe a tiny tear from my cheek and look up at him.

“Oh no.” He laughs sympathetically and hugs me closely. “Come on, Whit. Talk to Daddy.”

I groan and hold back a laugh. “Please stop calling yourself Daddy.”

“Hey, someone has to. I kicked my supermodel out for your sad little ass.” He smiles and shakes his head in that cocky yet slightly self-deprecating way that only Chase Kennedy can pull off.

“I don’t know.” I lean back and look at the person who I’ve told every weird and silly secret I’ve ever had. “I don’t even wanna say this. I’m gonna sound so shitty.”

He arches a brow. “Whit. Come on. We tell each other everything.”

“Like in fifth grade when we built a fort out of sheets and lay in it for hours, and you told me your dream was to play football on the moon?”

"Uh, yeah. That would be fucking awesome, and I haven't discounted it as a real possibility yet."

I smile and shake my head. "Okay, well. It's weird. I'm not even really that sad about losing Troy. Like, not nearly as sad as I thought I would be if this ever happened. I haven't felt super connected to him in a long time. I'm sad about losing the future I had planned. The marriage, the family, being a mom, and having a house and all that. You know it's all I've ever wanted. And Troy was always…safe. I thought he was the one who could give me that."

"Is that why you stayed with him for six years? You really wanted a ring that badly?"

"I sound horribly lame, I know." I sip the whiskey and lean my head back on the couch cushion.

He waves his hand. "Please. I stayed your friend when you joined the competitive Latin team in high school. Now *that* was lame."

I study his handsome, chiseled face, framed by messy hair and dusted with a light layer of whiskers. Even though, to me, he is still that wild, fearless, charming boy, I look at him right now and can see why girls fall at his feet. Chase really is *shockingly* attractive.

"I guess I just feel stupid for wanting to get married so badly," I admit, letting his presence bring on my word-vomit, as it always does. "He wasn't even right for me, and I was willing to settle just to achieve some silly dream."

"Hey." Chase nudges me. "There's nothing wrong with knowing what you want. You want to get married. I want to bang a girl from every country. These goals can't be achieved overnight, Cooper."

"You're sick in the head."

"You're the one who's so desperate for..." He wrinkles his nose as if the word tastes bitter. "Commitment."

"How did we turn into such opposites?" I ask, feeling spinny from the whiskey and lying down on my side so my feet are in his lap.

"No idea, Nit Whit." Chase sighs deeply and slumps down in the sofa. "You'll find the right guy, though. Hopefully, he won't be such a little bitch like Troy."

I kick him lightly. "Shut up."

My mind continues to race with thoughts and questions and fears. The future looks more confusing and uncertain than ever. Sure, I have my job as a nurse in the ER. Which I love. And I do have a place to live, no matter how eccentric my cousin Melody may be. But everything else is a sloppy, blurry mess that I never thought I'd have to face on my own.

Through all this, only one word surfaces in my mind and slips out of my half-drunk mouth before I can even think to stop it. "Sex."

Chase perks up, and he looks at me with shock and confusion. "R-right now? I don't know if that's such a great—"

"Not with you, moron," I mumble, turning onto my back to face him and laying my arm over my forehead. "I have to jump into a dating world I haven't even thought about in six years, and I'm so totally inexperienced. I barely even know how to do it."

"How to date?" He eyes me.

"How to...*fuck*, to put it in terms you'd understand."

He ignores the jab and sits up straight, looking at me with confusion. "Wait a sec. You and Troy never—"

I wave my hand to shut him up. "No, we did. Of course we did. But barely ever toward the end. And it was always so, I don't know…"

"Missionary?"

"I was gonna say *boring*. But…" I reach for the bottle and take another sip. "You're not wrong."

He flicks his brows and shoots me a quizzical look—a look that shows there's a little *too* much going through his mind right now. "He was your first, right?"

I blow out a defeated sigh. "Yup. The one and only. Point is, I'm terrified to get back out there, because I have no idea what I'm doing in bed. I'm twenty-eight, you know? This was not how my life was supposed to go, Kennedy." I groan, turning and burying my face in a couch pillow.

"Don't be scared of the single life, Whit. I'm telling you, it's the only way to fly."

"Maybe when you're a rich, famous, professional athlete with a ridiculous six-pack and a perfect fucking face," I say through sarcastic anger.

"Whoa there, pissy pants." Chase chuckles and jabs my leg lightly. "You're gonna be fine. You're gonna find your dude, and then you two are gonna have nice, clean, vanilla sex with the lights off once a week for the rest of your life. Boy…" He swigs whiskey and juts his chin at me. "Doesn't marriage sound great?"

"I hate you," I say, my voice muffled through the pillow I'm still clutching. "But that's exactly what I'm saying." I lift my head and look at Chase eagerly. "I want commitment. I want forever. But I don't want it to be so damn boring. I was ready to marry Troy without even thinking about how dull the relationship actually was."

"Yikes. You need to learn how to spice things up between the sheets." Chase bites his lip and nods in an annoyingly dirty way.

"It physically pains me to say that you're…right."

"So get out there and experiment. Have some fun. *Live a little*." Chase sets his massive hand on my thigh and gives it a squeeze.

Even when he's not flirting, he flirts.

"Easy for you to say. You're literally South Florida's king of the single life."

Chase waves his hand, leaning back and clearly feeling the whiskey almost as much as I am. "That's not true, Whit." His tone turns serious. "I'm *America's* king of the single life."

I laugh in disgust and kick him in the side. "I'm sleeping right here, I hope you know."

He stands up, looking messy and sleepy. His tired gaze lingers on me, and he smiles. "I'll get you a blanket."

To me, Chase Kennedy has always been an enigma. I've watched him treat every woman he encounters like some sort of conquest, just one gorgeous notch after another on his belt. Except me. I've meant the world to him for our entire lives, and I know he would never jeopardize that friendship. Neither would I.

But tonight, at three a.m., as my head swims from the alcohol and Chase turns around to get me something to sleep under, I let myself explore his unreasonably athletic body. Every muscle is flawlessly carved, and he carries himself in a way that makes him so irresistibly cocky.

For the first time in probably ten years, I wonder what it's like to be a Chase Kennedy conquest.

three

Chase

I hear Coach call a timeout as we're lining up on offense.

Thank fuck.

The Riders stadium is totally packed for our first game of the regular season, and the blistering sun scorches the field. With only three minutes left on the clock in the fourth quarter, we're down by seven against the Steelers, and damn, it's not looking good.

My usual home game hype is fading fast. I know I've been playing pretty shitty. Plays that are typically clear as day are fucking with my head, and I've thrown a couple of real piss-poor passes.

"Kennedy, what the hell is going on with you?" Coach Watson grunts as we pile into the huddle on the sidelines.

I bite down on my mouthguard and lean my palms onto my knees. Anger courses through me, and I know I have no one to blame but myself. "I don't know, Coach. I'll get it together."

"Yeah, you better get it together *fast*. The only way

we can pull this out is if you can throw a bomb to Sterling through the slot and get his ass into the end zone, Kennedy!" he snaps at me.

I wipe a drop of sweat from my jawline with the back of my hand and look up. "Yeah. I got it," I say through gritted teeth.

Confidence runs in my veins. I eat, sleep, and breathe being a quarterback. Well, that and getting laid. But I don't know what the hell is going on with me today. First game jitters aren't even in my fucking vocabulary.

I dig the spikes of my cleats into the grass and jog back out to the line of scrimmage.

Leo smacks my shoulder pad. "Let's bring it home, man."

I nod and stand behind Clay Rollins, the center, and draw in a deep breath, bending my knees and bouncing on the balls of my feet. If there's one thing I can do, it's throw a fucking football.

The crowd goes quiet, and blood pounds through my head as adrenaline rushes over me. Clay snaps the ball, and it lands softly in my grasp.

I pull it back over my shoulder and swallow hard. My eyes find Leo. Backing up and giving a couple of convincing pump fakes, I see him dart through the defense and right into the open slot. I jerk left, then aim right at Leo and send a powerful spiral racing toward him.

The second the football is out of my hands, an enormous linebacker plows into me, and I grit my teeth and take the hit. My shoulder slams into the grass first, and for a split second, it feels like it's tearing.

Fuck.

I get up quickly, only to see that the ball is in the hands of a fucking Steeler.

A pick? Jesus Christ. I'm Chase fucking Kennedy. I do *not* throw interceptions. I clench my jaw and let out a string of swears under my breath as I realize this game is over. We've lost, and it's entirely my fault.

I hate this feeling. I hate losing. I'm not used to it at all, and I don't want to be. I've worked my ass off on the field my whole life so I never have to feel this way. I shake off the pain in my shoulder and decide I just hit the ground wrong.

The Steelers run down the clock for the last two minutes, and I drop my ass onto the bench and grip a bottle of Gatorade, smashing it in my palm as I yank my helmet off and wipe the sweat and dirt from my forehead.

Dylan sits next to me and elbows my side. "Don't be so hard on yourself, bro."

I lean my elbows into my knees and kick the dirt. "I fucked up so bad. We needed to come out this season with a bang, and we got absolutely tossed by Pittsburgh. I should have hit Sterling with that last pass. We could have won if I timed it better."

"Dude, you gotta relax. We're projected to make it to the playoffs, no questions asked. It was just an off day. You're still a raw QB."

I stand up and sling my towel around the back of my neck as the game clock ticks down to zero. "I don't have off days, Dylan."

The feeling of defeat presses on all of us as we trudge into the locker room. Most of the guys are basically silent, and I slam my palm onto a locker when we walk in.

Coach keeps a positive attitude, of course, telling us we need to work more as a team and refine our offensive strategies and all this shit. But he really could just say, "Chase dropped the fucking ball," and no one would argue.

After our mildly inspiring post-game talk, I walk over to my locker without a word and start taking my pads off.

"Well, I guess the good news is that my wife is happy," I hear Leo joking with Elliot a few feet away. "Frankie will deny it, but she's still a Steelers fan deep down."

Elliot chuckles. "Hey, Jessica was raised as a Pats fan. I'm glad that didn't stick with her."

"Well, at least we have them." Leo shuts his locker. "Win or lose, we got our cute-ass good luck charms in the stands."

Elliot agrees, and the two of them seem to shrug off the loss pretty easily. A couple of seasons ago, they would have probably been pissed at me, or at least given me shit for how I played. Especially Sterling.

But now they just laugh it off and talk about their *wives*. Gross.

But as I hang up my jersey and try to shake off the frustration of this game, their words about having a good luck charm echo in my head.

Whitney was always mine. She went to every high school game to see me play. Well, she was a cheerleader, so I guess she kinda had to go. But she's always been my best bud and was reliably in the stands to watch me wreck shit on the field. And then in college at UF, she never missed a game day in The

Swamp. Sometimes she was totally hammered with her sorority friends, but still, she was there. And I never fucked up.

With her in the stadium, I played like a boss and just got better and better. That's it. I just gotta get Whit to come to every Riders game. And then I can get back to beast mode, and this shitshow of a first game will be ancient history when I'm throwing bullets at the Super Bowl.

I sling my duffel bag over my shoulder and walk out to the athletes' garage, feeling a wave of relief as the brilliance of my new plan settles into my mind.

Only problem is, I know Whitney Cooper. And I know that she'll say she can't commit to that because she's a psycho who works as an ER nurse at all kinds of sickening hours, and it's a big deal to change them. So I'll just have to give her something in return.

I click my keys and watch the door of my bright green Lamborghini Gallardo swing open and lift up. As I slide into the driver's seat, my slightly drunken late-night conversation with Whitney from the other day comes racing through my head.

She needs to learn how to do one particular thing that I happen to be very, *very* good at.

Now I just have to convince the only woman who is completely unfazed by my hot, douchey quarterback thing that she needs *sex lessons* from me.

It's always low-key kinda killed me that my best friend is an absolute dime and I've never banged her. So, I can't say I'm terribly opposed to the idea of being her "teacher."

four

Whitney

"You're getting your adorable little ass back *out* there!" Melody dances around the living room, flipping her bright pink-dyed hair over her shoulder and shimmying in my face.

"Mel, I appreciate the enthusiasm, but going to a party tonight filled with people I've never met and dudes trying to get into my heartbroken, vulnerable pants kinda sounds like my own personal hell." I pull a fuzzy blanket over my face and snuggle down in the sofa.

"Psh. Come on, cuz. You're not heartbroken. Troy was a total drip, and you know it. You're not even sad about him. You're just scared of being single." She pushes her thick, neon-green glasses up the bridge of her nose and raises her brows at me.

The truth of her words hits me like a sucker punch.

"I'm not going. I have a date tonight anyway," I grumble through the blanket.

My pushy cousin yanks it off of my face and crosses her arms. "With who?"

"The sexy Prime Minister of England, if you must know."

She rolls her eyes and flops onto the couch next to me. "You are not watching *Love Actually* again."

I pout and press my face into a throw pillow. "Please?"

Just as Melody is opening her mouth to give me another lecture about how many men would just absolutely *die* to be with me, there's a knock on the apartment door.

"You're getting that. Because I haven't seen you leave the couch today, and hello, Nurse Cooper, you're going to get blood clots." She pushes me and slaps my butt as I stand up.

I shoot her a look and trek to the front door, shielding my eyes from the blindingly bright colors on every square inch of wall in this apartment.

I yank open the purple door and draw back in surprise when I see Chase standing on the doorstep with a smile that definitely looks like he's up to something.

"Who is it?" Melody calls.

I smile at him and gesture for him to come in. "It's Chase."

She hurries into the entryway and places her hands on her hips. "Are you kidding? The *one* time I don't answer the door, it's someone hot and famous?" She shakes out her pink hair and purses her lips.

"Nice to see you, too, Melody," Chase says with a jut of his chin. "Let's go to the beach, Nit Whit."

I look down at my baggy sweatpants and oversize UF College of Nursing T-shirt. "Don't you have practice or something?" I ask him, narrowing my eyes with suspicion at his sudden interest in a spontaneous beach day.

"Just an early workout, so I'm done for the day. Get ready, come on," he says eagerly.

I stare at him with parted lips, now in a state of full-on confusion. "You're being weird."

"No, I'm being *nice*. You're all sad about losing five-inch Troy, so I'm here to make you feel better."

I sigh, rolling my eyes and trying to hide my laugh at his jab at my ex. "All right, Six. Give me two seconds, and…" I glance back toward the living room and lower my voice. "Try not to let Melody sexually assault you."

He cringes and laughs softly.

I walk into the little room where I'm staying. I shamefully have not had the time or energy to unpack anything, so the floor is littered with overflowing bags and suitcases that I stuffed aggressively to get out of Troy's and my apartment as fast as I could.

The memory makes me shudder. I dig through a bag and find a red polka dot bikini that I don't think I've put on in three years. I shrug and pull off my T-shirt and sweats, marveling at the fact that the swimsuit still fits.

There's definitely a little more ass and cleavage than when I first bought it, but I can't find the energy to care. It's just Chase, after all. He sees cleavage as much as he breathes oxygen.

I throw a pair of shorts on and walk back out to the living room, where Chase is being lectured by my cousin about how all athletes should adopt a vegan diet and how he just *has* to come do yoga at the new studio she's opening. He looks relieved when I smile and tell her to hush.

"Let's go, Six." I walk out to the front door and open it. "Bye, Mel."

"Have *fun*," she says in a singsong voice, standing behind Chase and giving me an exaggerated wink.

I follow Chase out the door and into the blazing Florida sun.

"Damn, Nit Whit. The titties are out. Love to see it."

I groan and roll my eyes, although I can't deny that the male attention feels good. Even if it is coming from Chase Fuckboy Kennedy.

His Lamborghini seems hilarious parked outside of Melody's very average-looking townhouse.

"We're walking, right? It's, like, three blocks," I say, holding up a hand to shield my eyes from the sunlight. "Not to mention I don't feel at all like dealing with your spacecraft of a car."

"Don't you dare hate on the Lambo." He shakes his head with disappointment as we start walking toward the beach.

The air is salty and sticky, and the radiant sun bakes into my skin as I realize I haven't gone outside since I got home from working a twelve-hour shift two days ago. I take a deep breath of tropical Florida warmth and let a smile rest on my face.

"You're quiet," Chase observes as we reach the scorching sand and find a place to sit down, laying out a towel to share.

I stretch my arms out and look up at the clear blue sky. "It's so sunny and nice out. Thanks for kidnapping me."

Chase drops down onto the sand next to me and leans back on his palms. "More like rescuing you.

That place looks like a rainbow unicorn yakked everywhere."

"Will you shut up?" I say through a laugh. "Melody is being a really good cousin. Although I could seriously do without her trying to drag me to some bizarre party tonight."

He digs his heels into the sand and looks out over the crashing ocean. "You should go. Get your ass back out there. Get *laid*, Whit."

I smack him lightly and shake my head. "I'm still so weirded out by the concept of sleeping with someone else. Like, what if they're really different? I don't know how to handle all this shit."

"I hope to *God* they're different from Two-Minute Troy."

I roll my eyes and admire the sparkling blue ocean and the rhythmic impact of the waves. Different is scary. New is intimidating. I like comfort and familiarity. I like long-term.

"While we're on this topic…" Chase turns to me with an eager expression brightening his deep-brown eyes and a dirty-looking half smile sliding across his mouth. "I have a proposal for you."

I narrow my eyes and turn to him, noticing tiny beads of sweat dotting his sharp jawline and defined nose. Something about the look on his face intrigues and concerns me at the same time. "What kind of proposal?"

"Okay, so I assume you saw how the Riders' first game against Pittsburgh went last Sunday." He looks down at the sand.

I swallow hard. I was working during that game, but I caught glimpses of it on the TV in the waiting room, and I know it was a heartbreaker. I also know Chase was pretty much responsible for a lot of the Riders' screw-ups. "So you're a little rusty. Don't sweat it."

He looks at me and runs a hand through his thick, dirty-blond hair. "I'm tryna be the next Tom Brady, dude. I don't have time to be rusty."

"You're coming to me with football problems?" I chuckle. "I'm a nurse, Kennedy. I can't exactly help you perfect your spiral."

"Okay, first of all…" He raises his brows and playfully taps my nose with his finger, making me jump and smile at his touch. "My spiral is already perfect. Second, I'm not asking for your assistance with throwing technique. I need you to start coming to the Riders games. Like, all of them."

I choke on a laugh. "Oh my God, you don't still think I'm your good luck charm or whatever, do you? Chase, we were in high school when that was a thing."

"And college!" he adds.

"Honey…" I offer him an exaggerated look of sympathy. "You're a great football player, but I didn't exactly go to Gator games for the sole purpose of bringing you good mojo."

"But the point is you were there. Sometimes drunk and highly distracted, maybe. But still there."

I shake my head slowly. "You know, I never really took you for the superstitious type. Besides, I would have to lose shifts at work. So…"

"So what's in it for you, right?"

I shrug and look back out over the shiny water. "Yeah. If I'm your golden ticket to a winning record, I at least deserve some sort of compensation in exchange for my highly sought-after services."

He eyes me, biting his bottom lip in a way that undoubtedly gets every girl within a five-mile radius at least a little wet. Except me. Sort of. "I'll teach you how to fuck."

"Chase!" I blurt out, the shock of his insane words hitting me harder than the scorching sun.

"I'm sorry, I'm sorry." He holds up his hands and lowers his voice. "I mean *make love*."

"Did you get hit on the head at that first game? I think you should see a doctor."

"Think about it, Whit. You're terrified of hooking up with anyone who isn't your lame-o ex. I can help you get more confident in bed. And the shower. And the car." He juts his chin at the Atlantic Ocean. "And that water."

I hold up a hand and shut my eyes in disgust. "Okay, I get it. It's pretty clear that you've lost your mind, so I'm gonna go," I say slowly, standing up and brushing sand off my thighs, my head still spinning from Chase's stunning offer.

He jumps to his feet and meets my gaze. "We've always helped each other out."

"Yeah." I snort. "With algebra and hangovers. Not with…*that*."

He inches closer to me, filling my nose with the scent of masculinity and the aura of testosterone that just seems to follow Chase around. "Yeah, well… we're all grown up now. There are new things to help each other with." He nods and gives me a smile, a hint of flirtation glinting in his commanding gaze.

I let out something between a laugh and a sigh and

tilt my head at him, noticing the way the sunlight bounces off his skin, making him even more handsome than usual. "You're losing your shit, Six. Take a nap or something."

I pat his rock of a bicep and walk back toward the townhouse. Chase is crazy! I mean, what is he even thinking…that he could teach me how to have *sex*? And that would somehow be a *good* idea?

I've always known he kinda wanted to sleep with me. But he's Chase. He wants to sleep with *everyone*. I'm his best friend, not one of his sleazy pursuits…

No matter how curious I might be about what's in his pants.

five

Whitney

"I cannot believe you're actually dragging me to this thing," I whine to Melody as we walk through the hall of a relatively nice apartment building, rapidly approaching the dreadful party I somehow got talked into attending.

"Will you hush?" she snaps. Her sparkly nose stud glimmers in the fluorescent lighting. Her makeup is colorful and bold and, well…Melody. "We're gonna have fun. *Fun*!" She shakes my shoulders aggressively. "What a concept."

"Yay, fun," I groan sarcastically. "I wanna be home by eleven."

We approach the apartment door, and I can hear the faint pounding bass of the speakers.

Melody turns to me and points a neon-orange-painted finger. "Don't be a buzzkill."

I force a wide smile and flip my hair over my shoulder. "Not a buzzkill."

Melody turns toward the door and grips the handle, pausing to look over her shoulder at me. "Who knows?

Maybe you'll meet the *man of your dreams*."

At some crummy apartment party full of strangers and Coors Light? Fat chance. "Yeah. Maybe."

Mel shoves the door open, and I'm instantly greeted by blaring rap music and a crowded, small apartment. People are mingling in various groups, all holding red SOLO cups. Everyone seems to be laughing and beaming with happiness, totally engaged in whatever conversations they're having.

I pull in a deep breath and hold my chin high. For all of her crazy pushiness, Melody is right. I've spent every weekend for the last six years doing jigsaw puzzles and rewatching *The Office* with Troy.

Melody rushes off to join a group of hipster-looking guys in the corner of the living room.

I opt to start with a drink and walk toward the kitchen.

"Oh my gosh, Whitney Cooper?" A woman's voice excitedly calls my name from the other side of the countertop.

"Beth Chang!" I light up with relief at the familiar face of one of my sorority sisters from college, and a beloved one at that. "It's been forever." I accept her tight embrace.

Beth is as beautiful as ever, with straight black hair framing her stunningly refined face and glowing skin.

"Way too long." She smiles. "You're, like, married, right?"

Her question hits me in the gut, and I push it away with a forced laugh. "Not exactly. Troy and I broke up last week, actually."

She gasps and hugs me again. "No! I'm so sorry, Whit. How are you doing?"

I finish pouring a vodka soda and swirl it around with some ice. "You know? Not actually as bad as you'd expect."

"You guys were together for an eternity." She reaches out and touches my hand.

"Six years. But it felt like an eternity." I laugh softly, and she joins me. "He just wasn't the right guy, so…" I shrug.

She raises her plastic cup and grins widely. "On to the next!"

I giggle and tap my cup to hers. "Amen, sister." I sip the mixed drink and remember Chase's insane idea from earlier today. I wish I could stop thinking about it.

I chalk up the incessant imagery to loneliness and, well, sheer curiosity, and shake it off.

Beth links her arm with mine and knocks back a good swig of her drink. She lifts a shoulder and winks at me. "Let's mingle, shall we?"

I shrug and lean against her. "We shall."

The party consists of mostly friends and coworkers of Jonah Chapman, the dude who lives in the apartment. Melody knows him from some yoga retreat or something, and the majority of attendees have a very laidback, hippie kind of vibe. The yoga-retreat crowd, I would assume.

"So what brought you here?" I turn to Beth, suddenly realizing that my sorority sister, who's turned into a sleek, buttoned-up corporate lawyer, doesn't exactly fit the aesthetic.

She flips her shiny hair and rolls her eyes with a soft laugh. "I met Jonah at some beach bar one night. We're just friends, but I'm kind of hoping it will turn into more. Do you think that's possible?"

I purse my lips. "Anything is, I guess." My mind swivels back to Chase and his dirty, *unplatonic* idea from earlier. Some friends can turn into more. Some should definitely not.

"I know, it seems silly. He's not who I expected myself to go for, at all. But, I don't know, feelings hit you when you least expect it."

I smile. "I would have pegged you more with…" I take a sip from my cup and scan the room. My eyes fall on a tall, dark-haired man wearing a shirt with the sleeves rolled up and square-framed glasses. "That guy."

Beth turns to me in disbelief. "You don't know who that is? That's Peter Chapman, Jonah's older brother." She lowers her voice and puts her mouth right next to my ear. "Totally sexy, totally loaded, and from what I hear, *totally* looking for someone serious."

I chew my bottom lip and examine the lean, handsome man who looks like he stepped right off of Wall Street.

Suddenly, I'm wishing I'd worn more makeup and a lower-cut top. "Should I talk to him?" I ask Beth, nerves lacing my voice.

"Hell yes, you should talk to him. That's some fine hubby material right there."

I force down the rest of my vodka soda and shake my hair out. That's the type of man I need. Steady. Stable. Ready for commitment as much as I am. Everything I *thought* Troy was.

As I walk up to this intimidating specimen of a person, a fleeting thought of what Chase would say enters my mind. He would tease me endlessly for my attraction to what he calls "cubicle guys," a blanket term for anyone who wears a suit and works in an office.

I shove Chase Kennedy out of my head and feel a jitter of butterflies as Peter catches my eye.

My chest is tight and nervous, and I know I have to impress him. He seems like the type of guy who needs to be impressed. I'm not usually one for exuding self-love or handing out résumés, but I force confidence onto my skin and smile.

"Hi there." His voice is deep and commanding. He looks at me curiously and extends his arm. "I'm Peter. The brother of the host of this *lovely* shindig."

I laugh and awkwardly shake his hand, wondering if I look as tense as I feel. "Whitney Cooper. My cousin Melody knows your brother, so she kinda dragged me here." I look down sheepishly. "Not that I'm not having a great time!" I add quickly.

Peter swirls his drink and makes direct eye contact, which only adds to the thick wave of nerves prickling my skin. I can't remember the last time I tried to flirt. I can't remember how. I mean, Christ, six years is a long time.

Peter raises his brows slowly and studies me. "You don't look like you're having a great time, Whitney Cooper." He draws out each syllable of my name as if he likes the way it tastes.

I sigh and glance around the room. The bass of the music thumps beneath my feet, and my head starts to feel a little fuzzy from the vodka. Or maybe just the giant piece of *husband material* standing in front of me.

"Need another drink?" Peter gestures toward the bar in the kitchen.

I shake my head quickly. I'm gonna need to keep as clear a mind as I possibly can on my first night out as a single woman in what feels like an eternity.

He gets another drink as I sip on mine, and finally my tension eases. I chat with Peter about random things. His job as a hedge fund manager. His family up in Ponte Vedra Beach. If he's a dog or cat person. He says neither, but I guess we'll just have to work on that.

I focus on trying to sound put together and eloquent. To not curse or make sex jokes like I constantly do with Chase. I think hard about the kind of woman a successful businessman like Peter Chapman would want to be with.

Minutes tick by as we laugh and chitchat, and I wonder if this could be it. Maybe I had to stay with the wrong person for so long so I could meet the right one…here…tonight.

I silently curse myself for the pathetic desperation screaming through my brain. I've known him for a couple of hours! Even still, he's so seemingly perfect. We click. He wants commitment and a family and forever.

At some point, Beth Chang comes over and says goodbye to me, giving me a nod of approval and eager eyes.

Peter and I find ourselves sitting on the couch, our cups empty. I've been so zeroed in on him, I didn't realize how much the crowd thinned out. Melody is curled up in a recliner, giggling with a few people and passing around what smells like a joint.

"So disgusting," Peter mutters to me. "I mean, aren't we a little old for *pot*? This isn't a dorm room, you know?"

I cringe to myself as I think about how Chase and I will occasionally light up a joint of our own during the off-season, watching *South Park* and laughing until tears run down our faces and one of us ends up ordering Domino's. "Totally," I agree. "So immature."

Peter holds his chiseled chin very high, everything about him giving off an air of superiority. I straighten my back on the sofa.

He looks at me with a blazingly direct gaze. "I would like to see you again, Whitney. You're a fascinating woman."

Excitement spirals through me, and I remind myself not to sound eager. "Okay. I would like that, too." Trying to match Peter, my speech comes out uncharacteristically formal.

"Trouble is, I'm jetting off to London for business early tomorrow morning. I'll be there for about a month, buried in paperwork and spreadsheets. It won't be fun."

I laugh off the note of disappointment settling in my gut.

"But when I get back, let me take you on a proper date. I'm very interested in getting to know you better."

I smile and look into his brown eyes, which burn with ambition and success and certainty. "That sounds dope!"

Oh God.

He chuckles in amusement. "Okay, then. It will be *dope*."

I curse myself again for not having a classier command of the English language.

Peter hands me his phone, and I program my number into his contacts, triple-checking that I typed it right.

He stands up and brushes off his khakis. "Better get going, though. Early flight."

I stand next to him. "It was absolutely wonderful meeting you." God, I sound like I'm eighty.

"Likewise, Whitney." He gives me a hug, and I take a deep breath of his expensive cologne and aura of success.

Peter says goodbye to his brother and heads out the door. As soon as it clicks shut, a relaxed and silly-looking Melody rushes over to sit next to me on the sofa.

"Okay, so…" She snuggles up with me and claps her hands excitedly. "Please dish. Now. What was all that? You and Jonah's suit-wearing brother were, like, glued to each other this entire night."

I feel myself blushing, but I don't care. "I like him, Mel. We're gonna go out when he gets back from London in a month."

She squeals and grabs my shoulders. "Oh. Em. Gee! From what Jonah's told me, he's super business-y." She squishes her face into a mock-serious expression. "Hmm, yes, stocks and finances…investments."

I laugh and shut her up. "He's successful and stable, and…it seems like he would be good for me."

"Well, that is just amazeballs, cuz." She hops up from the couch and reaches for my hands to pull me up with her. "See? Are you not so completely glad you came?"

I look skyward and stick my tongue out at her. "You were right, and I was wrong," I say with a playful eye roll. "But I'm actually exhausted."

"For sure." Melody holds up her phone and waves it around. "Already called the Uber. Let's wait downstairs."

I follow her bouncy pink hair out into the hallway, waving faint goodbyes to the people I didn't even get to talk to because I was so entranced by Peter.

"So apparently," Mel starts in a hushed voice as we walk down the hallway, "your Mr. Perfect has *quite* the history of lovers."

I swallow hard as we step into the elevator. "I know he's a bit out of my league, but—"

"Oh hush! No one is out of your league, my beautiful, amazing, brilliant cousin!"

I laugh at the flattery.

"All I'm saying is…the women he's dated in the past, according to his brother, have all been, like, insanely stunning models, actors, Instagram influencer-type chicks."

"Mel, I really don't want to hear about—"

She holds up a hand. "I know, I know. But *now*…he's looking for something serious. For someone real. That's you! Or at least it could be. I just want you to be super clear on something. He's had about the best there is in bed. Now I know that your IQ is double that of any of his past flings, and you bring a heaping pile of substance and realness to the table in a relationship, which puts you leaps and bounds ahead of any booty-flaunting Instagram model. But as far as the, um, *other* stuff goes… I know Troy wasn't the most…sexual."

"Mel!"

"Well, he wasn't! Just…you're gonna have to step it up, you know? Get a little *wild*." She shimmies her shoulders and bites her tongue as we step out of the elevator.

It's well after midnight, and the sticky Florida air melts into my skin. The palm trees glisten in the moonlight, and for the first time in as long as I can remember, I feel *excited* about someone.

As we slide into our Uber, Melody leans her head against the glass window and drifts off to sleep.

I look out, watching cars whiz by and groups of drunk people waiting for rides or walking home from the downtown area.

Melody's words play in my head over and over. *Step it up. Get a little wild.*

I swallow and shut my eyes. There's one person on this planet who can without a doubt teach me how to be unforgettable in bed. And his name is Chase Kennedy.

I mean, what are friends for, right?

six

Chase

The shower hums as I turn the water off and bask in the billows of steam filling the huge, marble bathroom in my apartment. Practice was tough as shit today, and my whole body is feeling it. I clench my jaw as the obnoxious thought of the Steelers game creeps into my mind and pisses me off.

My phone buzzes with a text, and I welcome the distraction.

Nit Whit Cooper: *On my way up, be there in 2.*

I have no idea what Whitney so desperately needs to talk to me about, but I'm always down to chill with her. I haven't seen her since the day at the beach when I proposed my little friends-with-benefits idea that didn't exactly go over as I planned.

I shake out my wet hair and glance in the mirror. I might have had an ass first game, but at least I look good.

Just as I pull on sweatpants and a Riders T-shirt, I hear a knock on the door.

I swing it open, and Whit waltzes in, wearing a look of determination.

I laugh as she plops down on the couch and crosses her legs very seriously. "Please. Make yourself at home."

"Smells like boy shower in here," she observes.

"Boy shower?"

"Yeah. You know how boys' showers have a specific scent because they use the same bottle of Old Spice to clean their hair, face, *and* ballsack."

I snort.

Her sparkly brown eyes are narrowed, completely fixed on me. Whitney's been my best friend, and nothing more, for my entire life, but I've always been able to acknowledge that she's completely hot. Her hair is, like, twelve shades of chocolate brown, and her body is completely banging.

I glance at her low-cut white tank top and dark jeans, so tight they look like they could have been spray-painted onto her toned legs.

I sit on the couch next to her and forcibly pull my gaze off her cleavage. I remember when she first started wearing a bra in sixth grade. I used to snap the elastic on the back, and it would drive her crazy.

I look up to find her gaze again and smile. "So what's up, Nit Whit?"

She presses her pink lips together and looks past me.

"I see those wheels turning." I tap the side of her head playfully.

Whitney straightens her back and turns toward me, her eyes burning with something I don't think I recognize. "Chase Kennedy, I would like to accept your offer. With the condition that I can set some ground rules for this arrangement."

I feel my eyebrows shoot up in shock, and I let out a laugh of disbelief. "Are you fucking with me?"

She relaxes a bit and gives me a classic Whitney look of irritation. "No, dumbass. At least not yet. That's my point. I need your help. And you need me, remember?" She points at herself and smiles proudly. "Good luck charm, right?"

"Yeah." I rub my forehead and try to process what is actually happening right now. "So you're serious about this?"

She flicks the back of my head with her hand. "Are you dense? Yes, I'm serious."

"What exactly are we talking here?" I smile and watch her blush. "You're gonna have to specify your needs. And once you do…" I pat my chest and jut my chin toward her. "Daddy will satisfy them."

She tries not to smile and makes a gagging sound. "I don't need sexual satisfaction, you degenerate. I need sexual…*education*. And not in the middle school kind of way."

"So no hand jobs in the back of a movie theater. Got it."

She squints in disgust. "You did hand stuff in middle school?"

"You *didn't*?"

She breathes out a defeated sigh. "My lack of experience would shock you."

"It's really a crime that you haven't banged more dudes. Like, a disservice to society. I mean…" I gesture at her flawless rack. "Come on."

She bites her lip in an attempt to ignore me, which only makes me want to tease her more. "Okay. Ground rules." She snaps her fingers in front of my face. "Focus, Six."

"I'm all ears."

"I want to set the boundaries and the pace."

"So no butt stuff until at least the third time. Noted. Continue."

"I fucking hate you." She covers her mouth with her hand to fight a laugh and uses the other one to smack my arm. "Be serious!"

I tilt my head and give her a teasing look. "Okay, okay. I'm totally serious."

She arches a brow. "This can't mess with our friendship. I don't know what I'd do without my best friend, and I don't want to find out. Whatever happens is completely for the sole purpose of me getting more…" She searches for a word, then lowers her voice to a more timid tone. "Wild."

I smile at the verbiage. "Getting *wild*, as you put it, will not change our friendship." I lock eyes with my best friend, holding her gaze and feeling all of the years of football games and messy nights and tears and laughter sitting in the space between us. "I promise."

She relaxes completely now, letting out a long breath and resting her head on my shoulder. We sit quietly for a long minute, her body rising and falling with mine, and I wonder if having sex will make us any closer as friends. I don't see how anything could.

"What changed your mind?" I ask her, unable to push away my curiosity for another second and knowing that Whit will for sure tell me the truth.

"Well..." She raises her voice to a high, girly pitch. "I just wanted any excuse to get nailed by *the* Chase Kennedy." She fake-swoons.

I laugh and shove her lightly. "Come on. If you just wanted my dick, you one hundred percent would have had it by now."

"Shut up. I actually met someone."

I pull away and grab her shoulders, grinning at her. "Already? Damn, you're out here moving faster than me."

"Hah. For once. But he's really perfect. Like, super stable, great job, wants a family, and all that jazz."

"All that Whitney type of shit," I tease her. "Yeah, I'm familiar. Well, fuck. That sounds awesome. So he's the dude you wanna impress with some magic skills in the sack, huh?"

"He's only dated, like, models and Instagram girls and all this crap. Like, he's probably used to having *good*-ass sex. And I'm, you know, not." She laughs in embarrassment, and I laugh with her, thinking what a damn crime it is that my smoking-hot best friend has never been properly piped.

"He's in London for a month, but we're going out as soon as he gets back."

I smile and study the excitement in her expression. "Plenty of time."

"That brings me to another ground rule." Whitney leans back and gives me a stern look, pointing a finger right in my face. "While we're doing...this...no other girls."

I fake a shocked gasp. "Nope. Can't do that. Sorry."

She smacks me yet again and rolls her eyes.

"Of course, Whit. Jesus, I'm not an animal."

She looks at me for a long second, as if to ask me if I've ever actually met myself. "All right, Six." Whitney stands up abruptly and swings her thick hair over her shoulder.

I get off the couch and stand face-to-face with her, unable to help but smile at the entire situation.

I'm gonna show Whitney Cooper how to do it.

She holds out her hand jokingly to shake mine. "Pleasure doing business with you," she asserts through a bubbly laugh.

"Oh, baby." I angle my head toward her and lean in close, smelling the familiar sweetness of her shampoo and catching the glimmer of intrigue in her eyes. "You don't know about pleasure. Yet."

Whitney draws in a sharp breath, and for a nanosecond I notice a flash of something in her gaze. She looks away and shakes her head. "I'm not some bimbo who's gonna fall under your magical Chase spell." She waves her hands dismissively. "This is strictly educational. You're still my idiot best friend."

She smiles lovingly and walks to the front door of my apartment. As she swings it open, she pauses and turns around to meet my gaze. "Oh, and Kennedy?"

"Yes, Whit?"

"This probably goes without saying, but…no feelings. You're still a living, breathing heartbreak."

Her words surprise me, and I draw back, laughing softly. "Yeah, uh, not a problem. I don't do *feelings*, remember?" I wave my hands around to emphasize just how ridiculous the notion is.

She shrugs without a word and walks out, shutting the door behind her.

I flop onto the couch and replay the last thirty seconds in my mind. *No feelings?* I mean, fucking duh. I don't *fall* for people. It's not in my DNA. And I'm sure as hell not gonna start with my lifelong best friend.

seven

Whitney

"It's open!" Chase shouts from inside his apartment after I knock loudly.

I try to push away the cocktail of emotions that swirls through me as I walk into the home of my best friend so he can teach me how to have sex.

In the past twenty-four hours since I officially told him I'm actually down with this unbelievably bizarre plan, I've wrestled almost constantly with how ridiculous the whole thing is. I mean, am I *that* afraid of being subpar in bed? So worried about not being sexual enough that I'm actually enlisting the help of America's most notorious fuckboy, who also happens to be my best friend?

The conclusion I've come to is…yes. Especially if I want to get a guy like Peter Chapman to fall for me. Desperate times call for desperate measures, as they say.

I puff out a breath, so wishing that *desperate* wasn't the word for my current state of life, but accepting the fact that it is, I swing open the heavy gray door and walk into Chase's glitzy castle of a penthouse.

"Where are you?" I call, locking the door and running my finger across the glass of a framed jersey on the wall of the entryway. "You've only been in the NFL for what, like, four years? Isn't it a little soon to frame your own jersey?"

"Never too soon to be a fucking legend, Whit." Chase's voice drips with a somehow endearing level of arrogance, even from behind the closed bedroom door.

"Please stop talking," I shoot back, flopping down onto the familiar couch.

I lose myself in the shimmering view of Miami at night, all the vibrancy and light bouncing around off the water and glass, creating an endless sea of sparkles. I lie down on my back and watch the fan spinning on the ceiling. I imagine what every other girl says when they walk into this apartment. The view, the floor-to-ceiling windows, the sheer *money* that seems to fill the air. Everyone is probably so impressed by Chase, so massively intimidated by him.

Sweet little Chasey from elementary school. I feel a sudden swell of pride for my best friend. He could tone down the ego, for sure, but he does deserve all of it.

"Are you gonna come out here, or what's the deal?" I call again toward the shut door of the bedroom.

The door flies open to reveal Chase wearing nothing but a pair of navy blue Calvin Klein boxers, hair ruffled, muscles…everywhere. "I'm waiting for you, dumbass."

I force my mouth shut and my eyes on his face, nothing lower. It's not an easy task. "Why aren't you…dressed?" I stammer, trying to stop my gaze from lingering on the package in his boxers, something I've been subconsciously curious about since I was, like, thirteen.

He stands with his back straight and all the confidence in the world. I mean, his body, yikes. Who would ever wear clothes? "Nit Whit…" he draws the nickname out slowly and walks toward the couch to sit next to me.

I inch away, suddenly feeling weirdly nervous around his biceps and his abs and…what's below them.

It's Chase freaking Kennedy! I scream in my head, trying to force myself to picture him as a skinny high school freshman telling me how nervous he was for football tryouts. But all I can see is strength and masculinity and…sex.

Chase angles his head at me and laughs in amusement. "We're gonna smash, remember? I don't know what kinda lame shit Troy was into, but *most* people take their clothes off for that particular activity."

I furrow my brow, suddenly feeling wildly in over my head. "So we're just gonna…" I study his half-naked body, careful to pick my gaze up after a quick second. "Jump right in?"

He toys with a strand of my hair, making my heart race a bit. "I mean, I figured we'd start with some foreplay. You know, maximize your education a little." He winks at me and drops my hair.

"I'm not ready to have sex right now." The words tumble out of my mouth before I can stop them. I feel a pesky burning behind my eyes, and suddenly emotion is swelling in my chest. "I've only been with one guy, and you're…well…you."

Chase runs a hand through his dirty-blond hair and half smiles at me. "That's why I'm the teacher, and you're the student." He nudges me playfully, empathy glinting in his brown eyes. A look that contains years of friendship and care and seems like it's reserved just for me. "What's going on, Whit? Did you change your mind?"

I swallow hard and relax slightly, remembering that amidst the body and the NFL stats and the fame, he's just Chase.

He's never even remotely intimidated me until now. Until I'm about to sleep with him.

"No, not at all." I laugh softly. "I just think we ought to start slower and work up to…you know…" I gesture vaguely in the direction of his crotch.

He looks down briefly, as if to acknowledge what's in his pants and the power it has over every woman he meets. "Like a…" He leans back, tracing the line of his jaw with his thumb. "Lesson plan."

"Yes!" I hold up my finger. "A lesson plan."

He chuckles and walks into the bedroom, pulling on a pair of sweatpants and shaking his head. "You're something else, Nit Whit."

I wrinkle my nose, frowning in fake sympathy as he joins me again on the sofa. "Sorry you're not getting laid tonight."

He gives me an exaggerated groan and eye roll. "I *guess* I'll survive." He sticks his tongue out at me, and I feel a wash of relief, seeing him once again as my childhood best friend and not the intimidatingly sexy professional athlete who has about a thousand times more sexual experience than I do.

"Okay." I tuck my feet underneath me on the couch and scoot forward. "Lesson plan."

Chase bites his lip. "We should probably start with foreplay. It's key. Trust Daddy."

I fake-gag. "New ground rule. No more Daddy. And I was thinking we could start a little smaller. Like…kissing."

He raises his eyebrows and draws back. "Should I teach you how to hold my hand first, too?"

"Shut up. I think we should go through the…you know." I gesture in a vague circle.

He furrows his brow and stifles a laugh. "The bases?"

I grin. "Yes. The bases."

He cocks his head. "Okay, Nit Whit. I'll teach you the art of lovemaking one base at a time. But, if you didn't know, I play *football*. Not that other lame shit. So we'll call them downs. First down, second down, third down…"

"And fourth down. I get it."

"Nah. *Touchdown*." He nods slowly like this is some sort of brilliant creative breakthrough.

I snort. "Then what's fourth down?"

"Probably off-limits for you," he says with a suggestive wink.

"Eww!" I smack his arm quickly.

Chase laughs heartily. "I'm fucking with you."

"So we start with kissing. First down. Haven't we kissed before?" I tilt my head and chuckle at a hazy and distant memory of locking lips with Chase.

"Uh, duh. You don't remember? Playing spin the bottle in Kyle Brown's basement? Seventh grade?"

His eyes light up with teasing enthusiasm. "You rocked my world, Whitney Cooper. Truth is, I've never been the same."

I flop back into the sofa cushion, smiling at the reminder of our spin-the-bottle peck fifteen years ago. "Oh shit. Yeah, I remember. I think I'm gonna need a refresher, though."

He grazes his knuckle across my thigh, and unexpected chills dance through me. "When are we starting this whole thing for real?"

"How about tomorrow?"

"You gonna pussy out again?" He nudges me. "No pun intended."

I narrow my eyes and shove him back, losing myself for a second in the depths of his brown eyes and the fact that I'm going to be having sex with him in a matter of days. "I did not pussy out, you jackass."

"I think you're just scared you're gonna fall in love with me."

His words catch me off guard, and I try to swallow my surprise. "Don't flatter yourself. The only people who will be doing any falling in love will be me and eligible bachelor Peter Chapman."

"Whatever you say, Whit. All I know is once you get a taste of this, you'll be hooked." He winks.

I wave off his comment. "Your ego should be in a museum."

"Some of the guys are at the Atlantic right now. Wanna go get drunk? I mean, if we're not gonna start fucking tonight."

"Yeah, I'll come. But only if you stop referring to sex as fucking." I stand up and rest my hands on my hips.

"Sorry. Banging."

I try not to laugh as I kick him lightly. My head swirls with confusion. One second, Chase is my idiot best friend who says stupid shit to make me laugh and never really matured past eighth grade. But one second later, he's…Chase Kennedy. No. 6. The superstar quarterback with a line of women a mile long and a six-pack that could cut glass.

I need to figure out how to stop seeing him as the latter. And I have a feeling that climbing into bed with him isn't going to help with that.

eight

Chase

"What's good, brother?" Leo Sterling smacks my shoulder as Whit and I step out of the elevator and onto the rooftop bar.

The Atlantic is pretty much the go-to private club for professional athletes and bougie people in South Florida. I used to bring Whitney a lot after I first got drafted to the Riders and she moved here because of a job offer at some amazing hospital. But once she and Troy turned into the world's most boring couple, she stopped coming out with me. It's damn good to have her back by my side.

"You remember Whitney, right?" I put my hand on her shoulder.

"Hell yeah! Kennedy's best friend." Leo, smiling like a kid as usual, wraps Whitney in a bear hug, which she happily accepts. "You've met my wife, Frankie, right?" He points toward our usual table, right along the edge of the rooftop. "She's over there with everyone else."

"Yeah," she says through an easy laugh, waving at

Frankie and Jessica and quickly starting toward them. "I'm gonna go say hi. Grab me a beer?" She glances over her shoulder, sending her shiny brown hair flipping around in what looks like slow motion. "Bud Light," she clarifies with a nod.

There's a spark in her eyes I haven't seen in a long while. That little Whitney Cooper energy is finally showing again, and I didn't realize how much I missed it until now.

"You know they have, like, *good* beer here, right, dumbass?" I call to her as she walks away.

She turns around and holds her hand dramatically to her chest. "Chase Kennedy, I'm hurt. Bud Light is the holy grail of beers. We agreed on this, like, ten years ago. If you turn into a beer snob, I don't think we can be friends anymore."

I shake my head and walk with Leo to the bar.

"You haven't brought Whitney out in forever, dude. I didn't know you two were still close." Leo leans against the shiny wood of the bar and turns toward me.

The perky bartender sees us and doesn't even have to ask what we want. She starts pouring two glasses of Blackthorne Gold, with her gaze staying fixed on me.

I jut my chin toward her, fully aware of the effect that I have on women. "Grab me a Bud Light, too." I turn back to Leo. "Yeah, I know. We've always stayed close, but she and her stick-up-the-ass boyfriend finally broke up, so she can be fun again."

He draws back and raises his brows, sliding a glass of whiskey toward me. "Whitney's single? Fuck, dude. She's been with that guy since the first time I met her the season you got drafted, right?"

I sip my drink and nod slowly.

Leo frowns at me and smiles at the same time, looking like he has some kind of big fucking question.

I set my glass down. "What, asshole?"

"Are you trying to lay the pipe with your best friend?" He lowers his voice and looks over at the table.

Whitney is laughing with Elliot's fiancée, Jessica, making animated hand gestures and no doubt telling them all some incredibly embarrassing story about how I cried during naptime in kindergarten or something. Which isn't even true. I had something in my eye.

I scratch the back of my neck, and Leo and I start walking toward the table. "I wouldn't say I'm *trying* to. But I mean—"

"It fucking kills you that you have a straight-up dime for a best friend, and you've never railed her?" Leo finishes matter-of-factly with a swig of whiskey.

"You're a cocky son of a bitch, you know that?" I chuckle and swirl my drink.

He shrugs. "Look who the hell is talking. I'm not an idiot, Chase. It fucking keeps you up at night that you've never hooked up with Whitney. You can't stand when women don't instantly drop like flies under your quarterback spell."

I pause and stop Leo, making sure we aren't in earshot of Whit and everyone at the table yet. "First of all, the only thing that keeps me up at night are the smokeshow models in my bed. Plural."

Leo laughs and rolls his eyes.

"Second," I continue, "Whitney isn't just some *chick* I'm trying to get with. She's Whit. She's a homie. She's *the* homie. I can't mess with that."

He smacks my back, and we keep walking toward the table. "Wow, Kennedy. I think you might be growing up a little bit."

"Shut it, Sterling." We pull up barstools to join a few other Riders teammates at our table.

"Where the hell have you been? I want my beer," Whitney whines. She's sitting between Frankie and Jessica, and the three have that one specific look on their faces that women get when they're together. Discussing dick sizes or whatever the fuck women talk about.

I narrow my eyes at her and hand her the Bud Light.

"He was probably fucking a waitress in the bathroom," Dylan chimes in. "Am I wrong, Kennedy?"

I lean back and sip my whiskey, glancing at Whitney, wondering if Dylan's joke pisses her off or even gets to her. If it does, she's not showing it at all.

I start thinking about our little arrangement again.

She leans over the table, exposing some perfect cleavage in a tight black tank top, and my dick wakes up a little bit. My mind races with images of sleeping with Whitney. My Whitney. I mean, she's not mine. But…in a way, she is.

I can't remember the last time I didn't wanna drink booze and shoot the shit at the Atlantic with my boys, but right now I kinda just want to get home and start our little…*lessons.*

Shit. Maybe Leo is right. Maybe I have been subconsciously thinking about how much I've wanted to bang her for the past fucking decade. And now I'm going to, because of an agreement. In all of my plethora of sexual experiences, I don't think I've ever had an *agreement* before.

But Whitney is Whitney, and as usual, she doesn't do things like anyone else I've ever met.

"Yo."

I jump out of my weird, thinky state to find Dylan standing next to me with an empty beer bottle. "What's good?"

"What's good with *you*, man? You're all, like, quiet."

"Just thinking about that game," I say quickly, grateful the response comes to mind before my dumb ass blurts out, *Thinking about why I've never banged my superhot best friend who's sitting right there, and also now we are gonna bang, and is it gonna be weird?*

Dylan nods toward the bar. "Come get a drink with me."

I get the vibe he wants to talk to me about something, so I knock back the rest of my drink and stand up. "All right."

"So…" Dylan lowers his voice and angles his head toward me as we walk across the rooftop to the bar. "Whitney."

"Yeah, bro. You remember her, right? She's been my best friend for my whole life."

"Other than me."

I snort. Dylan's not wrong. We got drafted the same year and instantly hit it off. He's really quiet and stoic and pretty laidback, a nice counterpart to my insanely outgoing personality. He's the kicker for the Riders, which basically means he gets endless shit from the rest of us about not being a real football player. But he takes it well, and he probably is my best bro on the team.

"What about her?" I ask as we nod at the bartender, who gets us another round without a word. Not without extended eye-fucking, though.

"She mentioned she's single now," Dylan says slowly, leaning against the bar and placing a cash tip on it. "I know you two are, like, basically brother and sister or whatever, so I figured I'd check if it's chill with you that I ask her out."

The phrase *brother and sister* almost makes me gag, considering our upcoming sex plans. My chest is weirdly tight. "Uh, I mean she's, like, *really* newly single. You know, vulnerable and all that shit. I don't know if anyone should really be trying to get in her pants right now."

Except me. But I don't count.

"I said *ask her out*, dude," Dylan clarifies as he sips his drink. "You know I'm not really one for casual bangs. I've always wanted something serious. You know, 'the one.'" He makes self-deprecating air quotes. "That type of crap. I'm not like you."

I swirl my whiskey and laugh. "No one's like me."

"King of the old rail and bail. Didn't you have 'Trust the name. Trust the pipe' written on your business cards? You know women have feelings, right, Kennedy?" He jabs me jokingly.

"Ah, yes, Dylan Rivera—the expert on women's feelings. I know, I know. Your parents had some kind of epic lifelong *The Notebook* kinda love story, and you think you have to wait to find some *magical* connection with someone. But, dude. You barely ever even talk about chicks. I mean, shit, you barely ever even talk at all," I tease.

He doesn't deny anything I just said. "That's

because I see them as more than just something to chase after, stick my dick in, and never speak to again."

"C'mon." I look out at the blanket of stars decorating the night sky. "I'm not *that* bad."

Am I?

I glance over my shoulder toward the table. Whitney catches my eye and gives me a tiny wave with her pinkie finger.

I lift my pinkie from the glass in my hand and wiggle it back at her. Looking back at Dylan, I'm pretty damn surprised by how protective I feel about Whit. I mean, for Christ's sake, it's Dylan Rivera. Aside from Daddy Elliot, he's probably the nicest and least asshole-y guy on the Riders.

But…fuck. I don't want him asking her out. She's my best friend, and I care about her. I don't want her getting hurt. That's the only reason.

"Nah, bro." I shake my head and pat Dylan's arm. "Her breakup is too fresh. Trust me, I know her. Just give it some time."

He shrugs as we start walking back to the table. "All right, man. Whatever you say."

"Yo…" Elliot drapes his arm around Jessica and sips his drink. "The new rookie QB… What's his name?

Dylan raises his brows. "Matt McKenzie? Kid's hungry. He's only, like, twenty-three and hasn't been on the NFL field yet, but shit…he's eager to get his ass out there."

"Oh, McKenzie. Yeah, I heard about him," Frankie chimes in, her voice high-pitched with excitement. "He's such a little nugget. Not to mention, he was one of the top draft picks from Michigan, had, like, over thirty-five hundred passing yards his senior year."

"A nugget?" Dylan chuckles. "Yeah, he's a damn good quarterback." He glances at me. His eyes flicker slightly, as if he's silently calling me out on my uncharacteristic quietness. "*Backup* quarterback, that is."

It's not that I feel threatened by this little Matthew kid. Because I don't. I'm *me.* But if I keep playing like complete ass, Coach is gonna give him a shot on the field. And he's chomping at the bit for that chance. I'm sure as hell not giving up my spot to some snot-nosed college star.

"Eh. He's all right," I add. "We'll see if he can gel with us."

"Shut up, Kennedy." Jessica laughs and flips around some blond curls, leaning into Elliot's massive shoulder. "You're just scared of someone stealing your precious prima donna spotlight."

"Jessica Randall. Never afraid to call me on my shit." I nod toward Elliot. "You picked a good one, Danes. But no, it's not about my spotlight. C'mon. I'm just saying we shouldn't get, like, dumb-hyped about some fresh little rookie."

Leo snorts. "Don't worry, Kennedy." He makes a fake sympathetic face at me. "You're still everyone's favorite asshole."

I roll my eyes. "McKenzie's small," I joke, hoping to divert some of the weirdly serious energy from me.

Leo nods and gestures toward Dylan. "Matt McKenzie could probably break you like a toothpick, Rivera. You're not even a football player."

"Okay, bro. Ha-ha, Dylan's only six foot. Dylan

played soccer in high school. Get your laughs out." He stifles a classic grumpy smile and flips Leo a bird.

Whitney's eyes widen. "You played soccer in high school? And you're in the NFL? Is that, like, common?"

Leo, Elliot, and I look at each other and laugh heartily.

Dylan lets out a sigh. "It's actually not that weird. Most of the best kickers in the league started in soccer. But these dickheads like to act like I did ballet or something."

Whitney taps her nail on her empty beer bottle and smiles at Dylan. "I think it's kinda cool. You're a professional in a sport that you didn't even play until college. Not many people can say that."

Is she hitting on him? No, she's just friendly. It's Whitney. She could make lively conversation with a block of concrete.

Right?

I clench my jaw, wrestling with something in my gut that feels wildly unfamiliar. Why did I get so butthurt about Rivera wanting to ask her out? Why can I not fucking stand the idea of her flirting with him? Or anyone?

I know why. It's because she's my best friend. Because no one will ever be good enough for her. Especially not me. I mean, shit, I'm the worst of them all.

I sit back down on the barstool and watch her fiddle with her beer bottle. The million lights of the skyline reflect in her eyes and make them spark every time she moves. Her body curves and slopes in a hundred soft and delicious places. I've never looked at her this way. I mean, not since we were, like, sixteen, and I was so horny I couldn't think straight.

But for the next four weeks, she's all mine. And I get to do things with her that I didn't even know I wanted to until now.

nine

Whitney

As I stand in the elevator and soar up to Chase's penthouse, I look down at my black cotton leggings that were nine dollars at Old Navy and pick at a piece of fuzz. It's barely evening now, but my eyes burn with exhaustion. I'm coming off a twelve-hour shift at the ER, and a particularly busy one at that.

Any other time like this, I'd be sound asleep right now with my blackout curtains covering the window. But today is lesson one with my alleged sex god of a best friend, and I'm pretty eager to get my little education started.

Only because I want to get good at all this stuff as fast as I can. Getting physical with Chase and, in turn, silencing the tiny voice of curiosity that's been whispering in my head for the last decade…is just a nice little side benefit.

I don't even bother knocking this time. I've been at Chase's so much in the past week or so, I'm getting pretty used to just barging right in. "Hey, Six." I practically sing the nickname.

"Nit Whit. Get your ass over here." Chase stretches his arms wide. He's standing in the kitchen with no shirt—shocker—chugging a glass of water. His hair is still damp from the shower, and he smells fresh and musky.

The Floridian sunset is pouring in through the giant panes of glass that surround Chase's living room, painting the room in an orange and pink glow.

Chase eyes me, and something in his expression makes me feel like my clothes are already off. He's never given me his token panty-dropping look before, but we've also never been about to do…this before.

I shift my gaze to the setting sun and walk over to the couch, flopping onto the plush cushions, feeling the weight of my work shift pressing my body down.

"Someone had a long night." Chase settles in next to me.

He has a certain energy that seems to follow him around. It's explosive and loud and wild. Even when he's just sitting on the couch, I feel it. He's magnetic. He has been since we were three years old.

Without thinking about it, I lay my head on his rock of a shoulder. "It was a long shift. But I'm here!" I feign overexaggerated excitement.

He laughs, his broad chest shaking softly underneath my cheek. "How bad was it? Anything crazy? Ax through the head?"

I roll my eyes and look up to meet his gaze. "No axes through any heads. Just a demanding day. Minimal blood and guts," I tease.

Chase wrinkles his nose. "I seriously don't know how you deal with that shit. I'd pass the fuck out, honestly."

I snort. "Well, maybe you're just a pussy."

He drops his jaw and looks at me, his deep-brown eyes bursting with his expressive Chase-ness. "Sorry, I don't have a weird affinity for injury and disease."

I flick his forehead playfully, noticing how we're inching closer and closer to each other, but not resisting it. "I have an affinity for saving lives, thank you very much." My voice comes out barely above a whisper.

"When you think about it, Whit..." Chase gently glides his thumb across my bottom lip, and I feel the burning-hot space between us getting even smaller. "Our salaries should really be switched."

I feel myself smiling, my gaze still locked with his. "That's an awfully humble thing for you to say, Kennedy. Maybe you're not as cocky as I've always thought you were."

He half smiles, sliding his hand across my jaw and behind my head, tangling his fingers in my hair. "I just act that way to get chicks. But you..." He pulls me closer.

I feel my heart rate increasing and my legs turning to puddles. We haven't even spoken a word about why I'm here. We both just know, and Chase seems to go from zero to a hundred completely effortlessly.

"I don't have to act any way for you," he whispers, his voice huskier than I can ever remember it being.

Suddenly, I get it. I've spent my life laughing and rolling my eyes at the gaggles of girls who follow Chase around and practically beg to get in bed with him. I've always chalked it up to his fame, his money, and his starting-quarterback NFL status.

But now, I'm sitting here with a pool in my panties

before our lips even touch, and I realize that he doesn't need any of that. Chase Kennedy is the human embodiment of sex appeal. I've just never experienced it for myself until now.

I've been missing out.

"So..." I say softly, not sure what I even plan on saying next. I'm not used to getting tripped up by Chase. I mean, Jesus, it's Chase Kennedy!

But then again...it's *Chase Kennedy.*

"So," he says with certainty, the syllable breaking my mental web of confusion and yanking me back into this moment, which seems to consist of nothing but him.

I lower my gaze to his lips. Those lips...I've watched them smile. And cry. And laugh. I've never kissed them, never *really* kissed them, and I'm suddenly wondering how that's even possible.

Unable to take the explosive tension that Chase has expertly built between us, I lean forward half an inch and press my lips to his. A million thoughts, many of which are dirty, swirl through my mind.

He draws back a second later and smiles. "Not yet, Little Miss Eager."

"But..." I stammer. "I thought kissing was first down." My whole body feels hot and shaky.

He places his index finger on my lips. "It is."

"Then why don't we just—"

"Shhh." He presses his finger harder against my mouth, which somehow just makes me really want to kiss him more. "I'm the teacher, remember?"

I roll my eyes.

"You don't just lay a peck on someone if you're tryna make it dirty."

"But won't it get dirty as things progress? I mean, this is only first base—"

"First down," he corrects.

"Whatever."

"Yeah, shit progresses, of course. But…the kiss sets the tone for everything. A little closed-lip peck says, 'This is about to be boring, forgettable, and average in every way, so strap in.'"

I frown and draw back. "Okay, then, *teacher*. Show me how to do it so it's…you know…" I look through the window and let my voice trail off.

Chase positions my chin between his thumb and index finger and turns my head back so I'm facing him again. "Dirty? Hot? Sexy?"

I swallow. "All of the above."

With his fingers still holding my chin, Chase takes his thumb and uses it to part my lips slightly. He angles my head back and slips his other hand onto my waist.

I try not to let it be obvious that my body feels like it's melting under his grasp.

It's just Chase.

A few burning seconds later, his mouth is on mine. Heat rushes through me as I lean into Chase's electrifying kiss. He moves his mouth slowly and rhythmically, every stroke of his lips convincing my mind and my body that I desperately need things I've never even thought about.

He slides his hand up my back and gives my hair a gentle pull, making me arch my back and sink my body into him.

"Now…" he pulls away slightly, leaving my lips begging for more. "We've kissed."

I swallow, searching for composure, but kissing Chase has me rattled to my core. "Mm-hmm," I manage weakly.

His hand slips under my shirt, moving slowly up my side, sending a wave of goose bumps down my spine.

There's no hiding the physical effect Chase is having on me. I guess he must be used to that.

"What's next, Six?" I run a hand through his hair, riding the rush of confidence that apparently comes with being kissed and touched and turned on by Chase Kennedy.

"Ready for more, are we, Nit Whit?"

The minty taste of him lingers on my tongue, and suddenly I'm wondering if I'll ever be able to see my best friend the same way again. In the way that doesn't involve heat and need and sexy kisses.

I draw in a breath and nod quickly. "We've barely even scratched the surface," I say, my voice sounding more like moans than words. "And based on that…I have a lot to learn."

"I can't believe you've wasted all these years not getting kissed right." His fingers are still tracing the curves of my body, making me shiver.

I decide Chase is like some sort of sex magician.

"Time to change that." He leans in again, kissing me hard. His hands are all over me at once, and everything seems to just make my body hot and achy and wet.

He reaches down and grabs my ass.

"Chase!" I jump, laughing through the kiss.

He smiles, his mouth still against mine. "Sorry. I've been wanting to do that since I was, like, twelve."

"You're nasty."

He slips his tongue into my mouth, lightly running it along my teeth and making out with me at a slow, steady pace.

My mind is hazy and foggy, and everything seems to be floating. He holds me tight, and in a swift movement, he shifts me so I'm sitting on his lap, straddling him.

"Damn," I pant. "You really are good."

He winks at me and dips his head low, kissing my neck, making me wetter than I can remember ever being.

"Kissing…" he says, his voice low. "Involves the entire body." He grabs my hips and rocks them against his lap, giving me a tease of his rock-hard erection. "Write that in your notes."

I let out something between a gasp and a giggle as he slips his tongue into my mouth again and deepens the kiss so hard that my whole body aches and squeezes, and my head is practically spinning.

Is this what kissing is supposed to be like? I guess with Chase, it is.

He pulls away for a brief second, and I fight the magnetic urge to get my lips back onto his as fast as I can.

"Whit…" He traces my cheek with his thumb, melting me with his sizzling gaze. "I've known you literally forever. And somehow…" He pushes his cock against me, forcing a tiny moan to slip from my throat. "Deep down…" His hands run up and down my back, setting off spirals of chills and heat and need. "I always kinda knew this would happen one day."

I push away the physical desire that's consuming my mind and roll my eyes, shoving my hand into Chase's painfully handsome face. "Shut up, jackass. I'm here to *learn*. I didn't fall for your magical spell."

He glances down and nods toward our hips, which are slightly, almost instinctively, grinding against each other every second. "You get that tongue technique?"

I bite my lip, looking through the window and leaning back on Chase's lap. "Yeah, I think I got it."

"And body movement, well…" He guides his hand down my side, teasing the burning-hot space between my leg and my desperate center. "That seems to come pretty naturally to you."

I tilt my head and shake away the fog of arousal, relieved that I'm starting to be able to see Chase for Chase again and not some kind of hypnotizing sex god.

"Yeah, because you're…you." I make a face. "You have…" I purse my lips and gesture at his sweatpants, covering a raging hard-on that seems to get bigger every second, and I somehow resist the overwhelming urge to grab it. "This."

He lifts a shoulder. "You surprised? The ladies don't line up around the block for six inches, baby."

Yep. There's Chase Kennedy.

I make a fake gagging sound and roll off his lap, slumping into the couch next to him. "Oh, now I remember. You're obnoxious."

He laughs and turns to me with a bright smile and raised eyebrows. "But you *did* forget for a second there. You forgot everything, for just one second."

I feel my expression turn serious, and I look deep into the eyes of the person who's been a constant, steady, *platonic* friend for as long as I can remember. "Maybe for just a second," I admit quietly.

Chase swallows, and I watch his Adam's apple bob up and down as he gazes out the window. "Yeah. Me, too."

Suddenly, he turns to me and lightly grabs my arm. The high of being that turned on, for the first time in years, still has my head swimming, and I jump at his touch.

"You're coming to my game on Sunday, right?"

"We have an agreement, Kennedy. Of course I'm gonna hold up my end. I already rearranged my shifts at the hospital."

Relief and genuine happiness fill his eyes. "Hell yeah."

"I'm just glad you got me those crazy-nice box seats so I can sit with Frankie and Jessica and all them."

"Duh, Nit Whit. I'm the QB. I got hella pull around there. They have to do pretty much whatever I—"

"Chase?"

"Yeah?"

"Stop talking."

He lets out his classic, self-deprecating, *I know I'm an asshole, but you can't help but love me* laugh.

I curl my knees up under me and lean my head back on the sofa, once again feeling the weight of that twelve-hour shift pressing on my bones.

"See?" he asks quietly. "It's not gonna be weird. Nothing's ever gonna change our friendship."

His words hang in the air, and something that feels like a thread of disappointment plays with my mind.

What the hell? This is a good thing. Of course I don't want my friendship with Chase to ever change. I guess I just didn't expect one little make-out session with him to hit me like a freaking train of sexual desire moving at a thousand miles an hour.

ten

Chase

I spit on the grass and wipe the sweat from my forehead with the back of my hand. The sun is blistering, and any concept of a breeze is nonexistent in the stadium during an outside practice.

"Quick-release drills! Kennedy, move it!" Coach Watson barks, followed by a blow of his whistle.

I shake my shoulders and start running over to the other end of the field to run the drill, trying to channel any drop of energy that might be left after this daylong practice. I'm hot and exhausted, but I look over and catch a glimpse of Baby Matt McKenzie. He rips one perfect spiral after another.

Fuck. I spit again. It doesn't matter how hot it is or how wiped I am. I have to give everything I've got, or Junior over there is gonna be starting before I know it.

I jog past Matt and the quarterback coach, keeping my eyes forward and realizing how tightly clenched my jaw is.

"Hey, Chase!" Babyface grins and waves at me way too eagerly.

Christ. He's like a high school freshman at his first varsity practice.

I give him a vague nod and keep moving toward Coach Watson, but apparently that wasn't enough disinterest.

"Chase, wait up, man." Matt is running to catch up with me, his lanky-ass arms still clutching the football like it's made of gold. "I don't know if we ever met, like, for real."

I squint and hold up a hand to shield my eyes from the sun. "I think it's pretty clear you know who I am, kid. If you wanna know more, just turn on ESPN."

He laughs obnoxiously, still following me. "That's funny. Coach says I need to start running passing drills with you. That's dope, right?"

I stop in my tracks and turn to look at him. His face is full of energy and shiny, like he's never grown a whisker in his entire life. I open my mouth and angle my head toward him.

He draws back in slight intimidation.

"Yeah." I narrow my eyes. "That's *dope*." I smack one of his skinny arms. "If you're gonna run drills with me, or even call yourself a Rider, you better start drinking protein shakes like water and living in the gym."

I pivot and start walking down the field again, but the damn puppy is still at my heels.

"I'm already on it, dude. I'm really trying to bulk up. Thanks," he says cheerfully.

I puff my chest and get right in his face. A bit more intimidation could do the little shithead some good. "You fucking with me?"

His eyes widen as he shakes his head vigorously. "No, not at all. I'm so stoked to be here. I've looked up to you since you took the Florida Gators to that national championship six years ago."

Good Lord, I don't feel like dealing with this shit.

I look him right in the eyes. "Are you trying to play football or get a fucking autograph?"

He laughs again. "Play football. But still, you're, like, a total legend."

Coach tosses me a ball, and I catch it, keeping my eyes straight ahead and wishing I could swat the little rookie away like a fly. Shoo.

Now I get to run passing drills side by side with him. Fucking yay. At least if I completely smoke him, he'll get the message that backup means backup, and he's staying there.

"Go wide, Kennedy," Coach orders.

I wind up to drill a long spiral. *I'll show you a legend, kid.*

As soon as I release the ball and it soars down the field with wild accuracy, I feel a sharp tearing pain in my shoulder.

Fuck.

I roll it around quickly. It must have just been some weird, leftover pain from that nasty tackle in the first game. I went down on it bad, that's all. Fucking linebacker.

Searing, sharp pain rips through my arm, and I grit my teeth as hard as I can. This is not happening.

I grab my shoulder with the other hand and press into the muscle, feeling my breathing become rapid with rage at the thought of being injured.

"You okay, Kennedy?" Leo shouts from down the field.

"Fine, bro," I call back.

I'm not injured. No shot. I'm Chase Kennedy. I don't get injured. But holy *shit*, my shoulder hurts.

I raise my right arm to throw another pass, still trying to shake off the tearing feeling that's somehow surging through my entire body. I push through the pain, determined to maintain my status as a top NFL quarterback and get rid of any possible threat of Mr. Second String.

Practice ends shortly after, thank fuck, and we walk back into the locker room.

"Dude, you're holding your shoulder a lot." Leo pats my arm as he walks past me to his locker. "You sure you're good?"

"Sterling. Come on. It's just a little tight, that's all."

He stands and looks at me with raised brows, as if he's waiting for me to say something else.

"Insert some dirty joke about the word *tight*." I wave my hand. "I'm too tired to be creative."

He chuckles and walks away, and I circle my right shoulder slowly, hoping the pain will magically disappear, but knowing damn well that it won't.

I can't tell my teammates, and I sure as shit can't tell my trainers or coaches. They'll sit my ass on the bench and get that prepubescent shrimp to take my place throwing the ball.

But I need to tell someone. A Riders doctor or physical therapist would rat me right out to my team. But what about…a nurse?

I feel a smile sliding across my face as I carefully pull off my sweaty practice jersey. Whitney will be straight with me about how bad this really is. I trust her to keep it hushed. She's always had my back.

Whitney is my golden ticket to fixing my shoulder and balling out this season. And I'm her golden ticket to mind-blowing orgasms. Seems fair enough to me.

eleven

Whitney

"You're doing awesome, Sky." I smile kindly at the cheery new nursing assistant who got assigned to my hospital wing this week. "I know it's overwhelming at first. And nowhere is more overwhelming than the ER."

The girl rubs her eyes and lets out a sigh. "I've wanted to be a nurse since I was little. I just never knew living my dream would be so…exhausting."

I dig my purse out of the cabinet in the staff room, feeling my own exhaustion from a long overnight shift pounding in my head. "You'll get used it." I laugh softly. "Kind of."

"Thanks for mentoring me on my first overnight." Sky grins.

"Oh, of course." We walk out through the swinging door. "It was fun!"

I fish through my purse for my keys and phone—which I haven't checked in hours. I see that I missed four FaceTime calls from Chase.

My heart flips, and my fingers quiver slightly as I

call him back as fast as I possibly can. He knew I was working last night, right? Something must have happened.

Relief hits my gut as the call connects, and his stupid smile appears on my phone screen.

"Hi, Nit Whit."

"Um, hi, asshole. What's with blowing me up? I checked my phone and almost had a heart attack thinking you were dead or something." I laugh through my quickly fading anger.

"I need your help." His tone turns serious, and even through the spotty hospital Wi-Fi connection, I can see concern flickering in his eyes.

"Oh, no, are you in jail?" I tease.

"Shut up." He rolls his eyes. "I can't tell you until you're in your car. Nice scrubs, by the way."

I smile and look down at my aqua-colored scrubs with little South Florida Riders logos on them, remembering when Chase got them for me as a present for graduating nursing school the year he got drafted. "All right, Mr. Secretive."

I swing open the door to my Honda Civic and slide into the driver's seat. It's still sort of early, but the car is already scorching from the morning sun.

"Okay, I'm in the car."

"I think I hurt my shoulder. Not torn, but definitely pulled something." Chase is whispering nervously, as if he's telling me that he robbed a bank.

I frown and study his face on the tiny phone screen. My gaze gets stuck on his lips, remembering the way he kissed me. Hard and fast and needy, like he'd always wanted to. Like he'd thought about it before.

"Whit? Did you hear me?"

"Yeah, sorry. Bad connection," I lie. "Well, why don't you just tell your trainers? God knows the Riders have the best sports medicine doctors and PT's money can buy."

"I can't tell them. I can't tell anyone. If I'm hurt, even slightly hurt, that'll mean bench for me and playing time for Babyface."

"Oh my God," I groan, leaning my head back against the seat of the car. "Are you still hung up on the whole Matt McKenzie thing?"

He draws in a breath, and I watch his face glint with a touch of something very…human. Very imperfect. Very *not* Chase. "He's good, Whit. He's good, and I'm…"

"Incredible," I finish, not sure if I'm talking about his football skills or his tongue skills.

"Struggling," he mumbles.

I press my lips together, feeling a confusing wash of emotion for Chase. I know he doesn't talk like this with anyone else. Not even Dylan or Leo. He never admits fear, or failure, or anything that might be perceived as less than cold, hard strength.

Except to me. And that's how it's always been. But now that we've kissed—not to mention, the *way* we kissed—something feels different. More raw and… intimate.

"You're a nurse. Just consider it…" He gives the camera a wide, exaggerated grin. "Part of being my good luck charm."

In twenty-eight years of friendship, I've rarely had the ability to say no to Chase Kennedy. Now is no different.

"Okay. I'll try to help you out." I twist the key in the ignition and shove the gearshift into reverse. "How about Wednesday?"

"I was thinking more like right now." His voice is raspy, hinting at something neither of us is saying, but we're both definitely thinking.

Second down.

I press my foot onto the brake pedal and shut my eyes, unable to hide the smile on my lips. "Chase, I'm exhausted."

"I have a bed."

I puff out a breath. I shouldn't even try to say no to him anymore. Not after that kiss. Not now that I know what's in my near future. "Fine. Wash your stupid sex sheets before I get there."

"I'm offended, Whitney Cooper."

I wrinkle my nose.

"See you soon." He flicks his brows up and down, giving me a playful nod.

"Yeah, yeah." I hang up the phone.

Pulling out of the hospital parking lot, I try, and fail, to push away the flood of images that overtakes my mind. I never gave two seconds of thought to sleeping with Chase Kennedy, but ever since that kiss, it's like my brain is making up for lost time, consumed with hopelessly dirty thoughts about my best friend.

twelve

Chase

"Shirts. You know they exist, right?" Whitney snaps after her eyes take a lengthy trip down my abs right as I open the door.

I look down at my bare chest and shrug. "Would you cover this up?"

She waves her hand dismissively. "Doesn't matter. You'll just be taking it off anyway."

I laugh in surprise. "Damn, Whit. You wanna at least come into the apartment first? I mean, I know our lessons are very exciting, but—"

"Don't you have, like, some sort of private VIP hot tub on the roof? I feel like I have a vague memory of you blabbing about that when you first moved into this place, and I tried to figure out how hard it would be to rob you."

I step back slightly, feeling even more surprise now. "Yeah, I do. You wanna go…" I point upward. "Straight to the hot tub? I mean, I'm totally down, I—"

"For your arm, dipshit. The heat will relax your

muscles and ease the tension in your shoulder. I wanna figure out how bad it is."

I bite my lip and let my eyes take a little trip of their own. Whitney is nothing short of sexy and adorable in her Riders scrubs, which somehow seem to make her rack look even more divine. "That's the *only* reason you wanna go in the hot tub?" I reach around her back and trace the slope of her ass with my finger, making her giggle and shove my hand away.

"Yes." She nods aggressively, trying to convince herself, but unable to fight the captivating smile that widens at my touch. "I am here as a medical professional."

"And I'm here as another kind of professional," I remind her, softly grazing her side with my hands. "It's as good a time as any for lesson two."

Her lips part, and I watch her eyes sparkle as the obvious crackling of tension between us burns in her mind.

She turns her head to the side, looking down the hall and giving me a view of her stunning profile. I notice the dusting of freckles that have always scattered her cheeks. Her painfully cute nose with a tiny slope at the end. Her giant brown eyes, always bursting with some expressive emotion.

"So, hot tub?" I ask.

"I wasn't gonna get in. It was for your shoulder. I don't even have a swimsuit."

I cock my head. "Whitney. You honest to god believed you were gonna go up to the rooftop with me and *not* get in the hot tub? When I have just *oh so much* to teach you in that very hot tub?"

Both my hands are on her waist now, pulling her toward me.

She leans into my grasp and laughs, letting her body press against mine. "Okay, but I'll have to just wear my underwear. And it's broad daylight."

My junk wiggles at the thought. I press my forehead to hers and smile. "You can just wear nothing. It's *private*, remember?"

She gasps and leans away from me, making me only want to hold her closer and tighter and harder against me. "We're not skipping steps in our lesson plan, are we, Kennedy?"

I look skyward and bite my lip. "No, Nit Whit. I would *never*," I tease.

Any other girl I'd have talked out of her panties and into my bed by now. But she's Whitney. So we'll follow the little game. But ripping those scrubs off and satisfying the decade of curiosity throbbing in my cock sounds fucking incredible right now.

I step into the hallway with her and nod toward the elevator as I lock my apartment door.

"So what did it feel like, exactly?" Whitney turns to me as a strand of chocolate-colored hair falls out of her ponytail.

"When I fell from heaven? Hmm. An old line. But a good one, I'll give you that."

"When you hurt your shoulder, you absolute dipshit," she says through a slightly annoyed laugh.

"Oh. Right." I bump my side against her as we get in the elevator and go up to the rooftop, both of us bubbling with laughter and comfort and the palpable buzz of sexual tension.

Getting physical with Whit, even if all we've done

so far is kiss, theoretically shouldn't change the fact that we're best friends. And it definitely hasn't. Somehow, it's made us even closer. And all I can think about is going further with her, pushing every boundary between friends and fuck buddies and whatever the hell else we are.

Whitney shakes her head with a laugh as we step onto the private rooftop deck above my apartment. "This is absolutely absurd. You have this all to yourself?"

I eye her as I climb into the steaming hot tub. "C'mon, Whit. I make more racks than I know what to do with."

She shrugs. "Better say goodbye to it all, since your arm is obviously dislocated, and you'll likely never throw a football again."

My heart jumps for a nanosecond at those words, even though I know she's just fucking with me. "You suck," I say as I slide down into the hot water.

Whitney stands perfectly still next to the hot tub with some kind of hesitation written all over her face.

I sink deeper into the water and raise my brows at her. "I don't think you can be my nurse from *so* far away." My tone comes out raspier and dirtier than I intend. I had my first little tease of her. Now I want her right here, with nothing on. I need to know what the rest of Whitney Cooper looks like. Feels like. Tastes like.

But I have to play her fucking game. Because it's her.

"I guess you're right," she says slowly, slightly above a whisper. Biting her lip, she reaches down and pulls off her top, revealing a black lace bra that cups the first pair of tits I ever really noticed. I remember thinking how perfect they were when I was, like, fifteen. Nothing has changed.

I smile and reluctantly pull my gaze away from her. "You're something else."

She laughs and rolls her eyes at me, slipping her pants off and stepping out of them.

I peek from the corner of my eye. Her legs and ass are just as delicious and incredible as I pictured.

"All right, Six. Here I am." She steps gracefully into the hot tub, and I have to hold my hands under the water so I don't grab her perfectly round ass, which gets remarkably close to my face for a brief second.

"Here you fucking are, Whitney Cooper." I draw my words out and inch closer to her. The water between us feels like it's sparking with electricity. "I always knew you were a smokeshow, but Jesus."

She looks down shyly, hiding her blushing face. "Shut up, Chase. You've seen me in a swimsuit a million times. You've barely ever looked."

She's right. But something's different now. We've officially crossed the line of platonic friendship, and I don't think I can ever see her the same. "I'm just sneaky with my looks. Now that we're gonna fuck, I don't have to be." I wink at her.

She groans as the heat of the water swirls around her neck, wetting her hair. "That's a nice, delicate way of putting it."

I run my hand through my hair. "I don't really *do* delicate, Whit."

Lust flashes in her eyes, and I watch her chest rise and fall underneath the black lace material that I can't stop thinking about pulling off with my teeth.

I swallow hard. I mean, shit, *it's just Nit Whit*. I'm acting like I've never been in a hot tub with a dime piece before. And trust me, I have.

Just not one who knows me the way she does. Who calls me on my bullshit and remains unfazed by my overly cocky, panty-dropping attitude.

"Okay." She scoots closer, sitting next to me, droplets of water sliding down her neck and between her flawless boobs—which seem to just be begging for me to touch and grab and kiss them all over. "Tell me if this hurts."

I nod, keeping my gaze fixed on her brown eyes, which get wider every second.

Whitney holds my shoulder and slowly moves my arm around in different ways, asking me to push against her hand and to relax.

"Shit." I wince as she pulls my arm up at an angle. "That hurts."

She smiles brightly. "That's really good, Chase. That means it's definitely not your rotator cuff. It seems like a minor sprain."

"So what does that mean for football? Is that little rookie douche gonna get my starting spot?"

She keeps her gentle fingers on my arm, grazing my bicep slowly. Her hands seem so comfortable on me, like they should have just been there all along. "Not anytime soon. The sprain will heal on its own, but you *have* to take it easy. I can help you with a little physical therapy to keep it strong and maybe get it better a little faster. I wish you'd tell your trainers or a coach or—"

"No. No one can know anything is wrong. And like you said, it'll get better on its own. Plus…" I dip my chin low and lightly touch her nose with mine, feeling her breath becoming more rapid the closer I get. "I have you. My nurse." I slide a hand on her waist. "My best friend." I run my other hand through her hair. "My…*student*."

She pulls in a tiny gasp as I grip her body harder. "Second down already, huh?" she manages to whisper through some very needy-looking lips.

"Hey, we're in a time crunch here. I'm trying to give you years of mind-blowing sexual experiences in just a few weeks." I run my tongue along my lower lip, watching her eyes glimmer with lust.

I can't hide my arousal, either. Her thigh brushes against my achy boner, and I pull her closer in response.

I've learned pretty quickly that Whitney has a special kind of effect on my dick. Maybe it's the fact that she knows me better than anyone, or maybe it's just that I've apparently been wanting her since I knew how to want a woman. I just didn't realize it until now.

"So…" I run a finger down her side and slip my thumb under her lacy underwear over her hip. "Second down is all about…" Sliding my hand around her butt, I give it a gentle squeeze, making her jump, then lean in deeper. "Touching."

She nods. "I think I remember that. But I thought second base was just boobs."

I shift her body closer to mine, getting two whole handfuls of her perfect ass. The water sloshes up between us. "Once again, we're playing football here, babe. It's a heavy *contact* sport."

I guide my hands around to the front of her body, finding the sexy little creases in her inner thighs and rubbing them with my thumbs.

"You are good at what you do, Kennedy. I'll give you that." She arches against me, her chest pressing against mine under the water, sending sparks racing to my dick.

"Whit," I breathe, hot need tightening my abs as I savor her soft, gentle curves under my fingertips. "You haven't seen *anything*."

thirteen

Whitney

My body reacts to Chase the way that you think only happens in movies. Here we are, in the middle of the day, in his ridiculous VIP hot tub on the roof, and every inch of me is begging and aching for more of him.

For Chase freaking Kennedy.

I'm way too shaky and needy and turned on to think about our history or why this might be a bad idea. I open my mouth, just inches from his, and all I can say is, "Show me second down, Six."

He touches his mouth to mine, lightly, taunting me with temptation. "Such an eager student."

The water under the sun is blistering, and my whole lower half is in knots.

Chase's commanding fingers trace and graze and slide all around me, and every second, I feel more electricity jolting me and pulling me against him like a magnet.

He's teasing me. Getting me absolutely, painfully, desperately wet. Must be some classic move of his.

I take a second to let my own hands explore, running them across his solid abs, gliding my fingers through the deep definition of his muscles. His whole body is tight and hard, and I wonder how I've gone my whole life without ever seeing him like this. I wonder if I'll ever be able to again. "You're unbelievable," I say through a gasp.

He nods at my hand, which is slipping lower and lower down his stomach. "You can touch, too. That's part of second down."

I swallow the fleeting feeling of sheer intimidation that comes with the thought of wrapping my horribly inexperienced fingers around Chase Kennedy's *famous* dick. But desire and, well, curiosity take over pretty quickly.

I slide my grip around his rock of a hard-on and feel myself jump back a little in shock and delight and pure heat.

Chase pulls in a sharp breath and positions my body on his lap so I'm easily straddling him. I'm still holding his dick under the water, slightly gliding my grip up and down.

"There you go, Nit Whit," he whispers, leaning into my mouth and nibbling on my bottom lip.

I can feel his rapid heart pounding against my breasts, and the water just seems to get steamier every second.

Chase grabs my wrist and slides my hand off his dick. "You gotta wait for that."

I let out something between a whimper and a plea.

He slips his finger underneath my panties and gently into my pussy, just barely grazing my clit.

I shudder in response, pressing my body against

his. “Shouldn’t you be teaching *me* how to do something?” I ask, rocking against his fiery touch.

“I am,” he says playfully, kissing me hard and sliding his fingers in and out of me, sending fireworks exploding all over my body. “I’m teaching you what you should feel. How you should feel it. So you never settle for anything less.”

His words echo into my mouth, and he moves his fingers faster and harder in magical spots I didn’t even know existed.

Okay, so it’s definitely not just a cocky act. My quarterback best friend really knows what he’s doing in bed. Or, in this case, a hot tub. And this is only *second down*.

He guides his fingers against me at the absolute perfect pace, and I feel my body getting hotter and tighter under the water. I’m completely straddling him, and his raging erection is only turning me on more.

“Holy shit, Chase,” I moan, arching and leaning against him, my pussy squeezing his fingers.

I open my eyes, and the whole world is blurry. I see his half smile. He’s clearly pleased with what he’s doing. His brown eyes are wide with lust. I drop my head back as my toes curl and my thighs grip him and I come. My mind is filled with stars and explosions, and nothing else in the entire world matters except for Chase Kennedy’s unbelievably skilled hand.

I can barely catch my breath as I lean forward, slumping my head against his broad shoulder, letting my body float in the water.

“That was…” I pant. My heart is still slamming in my chest. “I’ve never come like that.” My words sound slurred.

Chase holds my waist tightly, running his hands over my skin, still sending chills through me. "Yeah, I'll bet you haven't." He clenches his jaw. "And it's a fucking crime, because you're sexy as all hell. You're beautiful, Whitney. I don't tell you that enough."

I lift my head and smile at him, resting my forehead on his. "Why would you ever tell me that, Six? We've spent more than two decades ragging on each other constantly. And you said nothing would change between us."

"I can tell my best friend that she's beautiful. And it can have absolutely nothing to do with the fact that I just gave her probably the hottest orgasm I've ever seen."

I laugh and slide off his lap, toying with the bubbly water and still reeling from the bursting pleasure buzzing through my body. "I don't know if I've ever heard you say the word *beautiful*."

Chase turns to me, his gaze piercing. "Until I watched you—felt you—experience something like that for the first time, I don't think I've ever seen anything that really was."

I furrow my brow and laugh, trying to lighten the mood. Something resembling butterflies is flurrying in my belly, and looking at Chase is making it more intense. I keep wanting to kiss him. I keep accidentally seeing him as something other than the boy down the street who's been my best friend since I can remember.

I wave off his comment. "Oh hush. Why?"

He looks down and bites his lip, suddenly aware of the not-so-playful-and-friendly mood and quickly making an effort to fix it. "'Cause, Whit. I've just always wanted to make you squirm. I guess it's been silently pissing me off for all these years that you're the only girl I've never gotten to go absolutely *crazy*. And now I have." He leans back and grins proudly.

I splash water in his face. "Shut up, asshole."

"So, did you learn something in today's class?" He pinches my side playfully, and I laugh and wiggle away from him.

I learned what a real, hard, mind-blowing orgasm feels like, and I can't imagine anyone else doing it like you. I learned I need to be a little more careful about falling under the magic Chase spell I thought I was immune to.

"Yeah, Six. I learned something."

fourteen

Whitney

"I've barely seen you lately, and I freaking *miss* you," Melody whines from outside my bedroom door.

"I know, Mel." I wiggle into a clean set of scrubs and dig around for some socks. As much as this tiny room has started to feel like home, it sure does get cluttered fast. "I'll be right out," I shout, hopping on one foot to shove a sneaker on.

"You don't have to leave for the hospital for ten minutes," Melody asserts. "So I'm making us coffee, and we're hanging out."

I smile and swing the door open, meeting her neon-pink hair and pouty eyes. "For ten minutes?" I ask with a smile.

"I will take what I can get." She gives her hair a sassy flip and bounces toward the kitchen.

I bend over to twist my hair into a ponytail and smooth out my pants. The kitchen is warm and smells like hazelnut and vanilla from whatever fancy coffee Melody is brewing. Christmas lights are strung all over the open shelves and taped along the ceiling, and there's hardly a surface that doesn't have at least one potted succulent plant on it.

I lean against the countertop and take the steaming mug from my cousin. "Thanks, Mel."

"I mean, okay. I get that you're, like, saving lives in the emergency room and all that. But I know you haven't been working *double* your usual shifts. And you've been at Chase's a lot."

I swallow and sip my coffee, knowing exactly what's coming next.

"And don't get me wrong. Chase Kennedy…I mean…" She fans herself and holds her hand to her chest. "He's a catch and a half. But I also know he's a *notorious* fuckboy. But you have to know even more about that than I do! He's your best friend. And trust me, sleeping with him can and will ruin that."

I take a deep breath and glance at the clock. I knew Nosy Mel couldn't stay out of my business for much longer, especially where Chase is concerned. "I'm not sleeping with him, Melody."

Not yet, anyway.

She arches a defined eyebrow that sports a sparkly piercing. "Very funny, cuz. I know an orgasm glow when I see one. And from what I can tell about Chase… he'll get you about as vibrant as the damn sun."

I hold my mug against my lip, trying and failing to hide my smile at the image of the hot tub. "I told you, I want to go after Peter Chapman."

"The Wall Street guy from Jonah's apartment party, right? I kinda forgot about him." She giggles.

"Well, I didn't. He's taking me out as soon as he gets back from London in a couple weeks, and I have a really good feeling about it. He's stable, Mel. He wants commitment and a family and something real. Something lifelong."

"Something that Chase Kennedy doesn't want," she says matter-of-factly, locking her gaze with mine.

I wave my hand dismissively and take another swig of coffee. "What does Chase have to do with any of this? He's my childhood best friend. Nothing more."

"Then explain the glow." She sets her coffee mug on the countertop and crosses her arms, leaning close to me. "Explain. The. Glow."

I bite my lip, staring into my coffee and knowing I'm absolutely miserable at keeping secrets. Besides, I *live* with Melody. And she apparently has some sixth sense for sexual satisfaction.

I lower the cup. "Okay, but you better be completely chill about this. No screaming or jumping or making any kind of deal."

Her eyes widen with excitement, and she makes an exaggerated lip-zipping motion. "Remaining calm. Got it."

"Chase is kind of…" I fiddle with a bulb on one of the twinkly strings of lights, trying to find the easiest way to explain our agreement without sounding completely insane. "Teaching me some things. Like… physical things."

She gasps and grins widely. "So you *are* sleeping together. I freaking knew it, Whitney!" Melody's voice is something between a whisper and a squeal.

"Well, no, not yet. That's the last lesson. We have a little plan. But we've done a couple other things, so I guess that explains the…" I circle my hand in front of my face sarcastically. "*Glow*."

"That's so adorable, oh my Lordy!" Melody squeezes her hands together. "Teaching you how to bang? Wow. That's the cutest thing *ever.* I always knew you two would figure your shit out and end up together."

My chest tightens. "No, Mel. We're not together. We're—"

"Oh." She flicks her hand and finishes her coffee. "No label yet, of course. I mean, it's so new, and he's, like, totally famous. So you guys wanna keep it on the ol' down low. I got you, girl!"

"No." I shake my head. "Listen to me. We're not together, and we're not ever going to be. This is Chase we're talking about. Chase. My best friend since forever who also happens to be a world-class NFL quarterback and has a bedroom full of exotic-looking supermodels every weekend."

She frowns and draws back. "But you guys are getting all…physical. That has to mean something."

"It doesn't mean anything." The words crash around me, harsh and cold and true. "It's exactly what I said it is. He's showing me my way around the bedroom so I'm ready for the dating world. For *Peter*, remember?"

"Oh. You're serious about him?"

I groan in frustration. "Yes, Melody. I'm very serious about him. And I don't want to be some stupidly inexperienced child when it comes to sex, so Chase is helping me out. As a *friend.*"

The corners of her mouth turn down. "That's a terrible idea."

I roll my eyes and rinse my mug in the sink, checking the clock again. "Thanks for the support."

"I'm looking out for you, Whit. I know how this kinda stuff works. He's gonna show you his undoubtedly magical and totally mind-blowing tricks between the sheets, and you're gonna fall in love with him. No, scratch that. You're going to realize that you've *been* in love with him since you were thirteen."

I shut off the faucet and press my fingers into my temples. "Melody, I appreciate you caring about me. But I'm *fine.* I know Chase inside out and upside down. Were always gonna be friends. And no one will be doing any falling, I can assure you. I mean, come on. If I were going to suddenly realize I'm in love with my best friend, don't you think it would have happened by now?"

"Sex changes everything. And from what I imagine getting nailed by Chase Kennedy is like…that's gotta be some classic 'fuck me so good I fall in love with you' sex. Not to mention, you're already closer to him than anyone else. You better have some sturdy emotional walls up."

I walk to the little entryway of the townhouse and grab my purse off the hooks by the door, swinging it over my shoulder and rummaging for my keys. "Just trust me, Melody. There are no feelings that aren't completely platonic. And maybe a little physical, but just for a couple weeks. The thought of anything romantic with Chase seems completely ridiculous. He doesn't even know what romance is."

Melody shouts after me as I'm walking out the door, "But I take it he's good with his hands?"

I laugh and shake my head as I shut the door, walking through the burning heat to my car. The air is sticky and salty, and the palm trees around the townhouses sway lightly in the breeze. As I unlock my Honda and slide into the driver's seat, I pull out my phone to send Chase a text. Chase. My *friend.*

Careful with that shoulder at your workout today. xo

I don't hit send just yet and stare at the screen for a long second, finally clicking the delete button with my thumb a couple times.

Careful with that shoulder at your workout today!

That's better. Nice and platonic.

fifteen

Chase

I feel my phone buzz in my pocket as I'm walking into the Riders training center. I glance at it and smile at a text from Whit. Just looking at her name on the screen sends flashes of the other day in the hot tub racing through my mind.

God, she was hot and tight and wet. Touching her and feeling her and hearing her moan my name was everything I didn't know I needed from Whitney Cooper.

I knew this game we're playing would be fun. I just didn't know quite how much.

"Kennedy! Come here for a second," Coach Watson shouts from across the weight-training area.

Fuck. He knows about my shoulder.

I play it cool and stand up as straight as I can. "What's up, Coach?"

"I want you to start working with Matt McKenzie a bit. Get him throwing pro-level passes."

Why? So he can take my starting spot? Not a chance.

"Uh, Coach, not to be an ass about it, but isn't that what the quarterback coach is for?" I nod toward Coach Groff, who's been the main QB coordinator since I first got drafted.

"Generally, yes." Coach Watson crosses his arms. "And Groff is still doing the majority of the work with both of you. But the hands-on experience you have with this offense is our most valuable asset in grooming him."

I have to physically stop myself from groaning. "With all due respect, Coach, I don't get paid to help rookies."

He raises his brows at me and chuckles in a weirdly intimidating way. "But I get paid to tell you what to do. Don't be a prima donna, Kennedy. You're getting too mature for all the stardom and showboating, all the cocky bullshit. Come on. You're one of the best QB's in the league. Use that for more than just Nike commercials and getting laid."

I clench my jaw and look over at the rookie, who's struggling to bench-press some embarrassingly low amount of weight. I guess as long as I'm helping him, I'm resting my shoulder, which Whit said is the most important thing to get it better. Besides, the kid looks at me like I walk on fucking water. Not that I need the ego boost, but I'll take the admiration.

"Shit," Matt grunts as he racks the wobbly bar.

I roll my eyes and look back at Coach Watson. "All right. I'll give him some pointers."

Coach pats my back. "Good, Kennedy. Thanks."

I nod at him and start walking over to McKenzie, who's sitting up on the bench, stretching his arms.

"Chase! Hey, man." He grins at me and stands

suddenly, like he's about to shake my hand or some shit.

I laugh softly. "At ease, Junior. I'm gonna help you with some Riders offenses and shit."

"You are?" His eyes light up as he chuckles with surprise.

"Yeah, well, since you clearly have the weight-training thing down." I glance at the measly weights on either side of the bar. "What are you ripping? Like, three hundred?" I tease him.

He laughs nervously and looks down at the floor. "Not exactly. I always just kind of relied on my arm. It got me through college and to the draft. And now here. But can I tell you something?"

I sit on the bench next to his with my legs on either side of it. "I'm guessing you're just gonna say it."

"I feel like I'm so in over my head. I was a solid college QB at Michigan. College football made sense to me. I felt like nothing could faze me on that field. But here…"

I smile. "That's right, kid. This isn't college anymore. The pros are a different fucking level. Trust me. I played half my college games hungover and was still one of the top draft picks for the NFL. My arm was all I needed. But not here. The pros are as much a mental game as they are physical. You just have to remember that you're the absolute best there is. And you're playing with the best offense there is. If you can throw it, they'll catch it. It's all on you."

"That kinda makes it worse. Besides, *you're* the best there is. I'm your backup," he says with a meager shrug.

For now.

"That's a bullshit attitude if I ever heard one. Now quit being a pussy." I stand up and walk behind his bench, adding a couple of weights to either side of the bar. "I'll spot you."

Matt nervously holds the bar and bench-presses the weight slowly. I don't really give a fuck about the fact that I'm helping out the rookie. I'm just glad my shoulder is getting a break.

He does a couple reps before grunting and racking the bar again. "I don't know, man." He runs a hand through his hair and leans forward. "I'm no superstar."

"Dude, you're a South Florida Rider."

"That's easy for you to say. Your entire persona fits exactly what it should be." He looks up at me. "I've heard about the cheerleader three-ways. You're a legend, and you still have so many good years. You have a household name that's synonymous with peak athleticism and talent. Not to mention the *women*."

I laugh and wave my hand. "You were a big deal in the draft. We all heard about you. You'll get to my level, Junior. And the women…the women will come, trust me. In more ways than one." I shoot him a wink.

His face flushes slightly at that comment. "Thanks, Chase. I really appreciate you mentoring me, or whatever. I know how to be a quarterback, just not like you. Not like a pro."

"It's a hell of a lot more than throwing a football. Which you can still get better at." I stand up to go start the ab circuit my trainers planned for me today.

"You'll help me, though?" Babyface calls after me.

I roll my eyes and turn around, half smiling at him. The poor kid really does need me. "Yeah, yeah. I'll take you through some offenses after my workout."

"Dope!"

I hold out my arm and point at him as I back away. "Step one to being a professional quarterback—don't say 'dope.'"

He shakes his head and smiles. "But I've heard you say that."

I pat my chest and arch a brow at him. "Dude. I'm *me*."

I walk into the other room to get started on my ab sets and pull out my phone. Whitney's text is still on my home screen, and I read it again, then type a response.

Don't worry. I'm taking it easy. Mostly hitting abs.

I slide it back into my pocket and feel it buzz with an answer almost instantly.

Thank God. I was wondering when you were gonna fix that six-pack situation.

I smile and laugh softly.

"What are you smiling at like some fucking middle schooler?" Dylan walks past me and smacks my back with his towel.

"Just some needy chick asking for a booty call for later tonight." I slip the phone back into my pocket.

"Ah. A day in the life."

"What are you even doing here, bitchboy? Don't you have a soccer game to play or something?" I squat down and sit on a mat, waiting for a trainer and being careful not to put any weight on my right arm.

Dylan sits on the mat next to me. "You know you have, like, five jokes, right? You just recycle them constantly?"

I angle my head toward him. "C'mon, dude. I have at least seven. Give me some credit."

Dylan lies on his back to stretch and looks at me. "How's your hot friend doing? Whitney?"

The question catches me off guard. I wonder if he's figured it out. Aside from Whitney herself, Dylan can probably read me better than anyone else. Not that I'm particularly difficult to read, but still.

"She's fine, man. She's good." I keep my gaze forward, but I can sense Dylan narrowing his eyes at me.

"You're telling me you're *not* hitting that. You. Chase Kennedy. Womanizer of the first order. You're letting your ten-out-of-ten newly single best friend stay out of your bedroom? Who are you?"

I bite my lip and start ripping some sit-ups. "It's complicated, Rivera."

"Ah." He starts matching me sit-up for sit-up, so I speed up my pace to show him up, because, well, I have to. "The truth comes out. Hey, man, maybe she's the one? You ever think of that? I mean, she's been a huge part of your life for, like, ever."

I laugh loudly and grab a medicine ball from the rack next to me. "The one? Dude. Are you forgetting who you're talking to? There's no such thing as the one. There are hot girls, and there's my dick. And those things just seem to go together."

Dylan shakes his head, clearly determined to get me to say the most asshole-ish things I can possibly think of. "Everyone has a one, Kennedy."

"Okay, Cinderella. I'm gonna knock out these ab sets just in case I happen to find the *one* at a bar next weekend."

Damn Rivera and his destiny-love garbage. I hate thinking about shit like that. It makes me think about my parents, which just reminds me that it's all BS anyway. *True love*, my ass.

Whitney sort of buys into all that stuff. Which is why she wants a guy like Accountant Peter. Which is why she will never, ever want someone like me.

sixteen

Whitney

"Watch the safety, moron! We talked about this!" Frankie Sterling jumps up from her seat in the box section of the stadium and yells into the glass at her husband, Leo, who just got tackled pretty bad.

"Bless their hearts, they might lose this one." Erica Anderson, the tiny blonde and adorably flawless wife of AJ Anderson, holds her hand to her chest. "My AJ hates to lose, I'll tell you that."

Frankie slumps down in her seat and toys with a plastic ring hanging from a chain around her neck. "Our men sure do hate to lose, don't they? Those damn alphas."

I smile and sip a fruity drink. Chase told me he'd get me great VIP tickets with the players' families when I agreed to show up to every game, but he didn't mention they'd be full-on suites with drink service and air conditioning.

Unfortunately, I don't seem to be succeeding in my role as the QB's good luck charm. They're down by seven against the Broncos, and there's only two minutes left in the fourth quarter.

"But what if Trash is hungry, Mommy?" I hear Asher's timid voice whining softly.

"He'll be fine, bud. We fed him before we left, and he'll get another meal after Daddy's game is over." Jessica, new wife of running back Elliot Danes and stepmom to his adorable six-year-old, leans over and kisses Asher's forehead.

"I think Daddy's gonna lose," Asher asserts, staring out at the field and pressing his hands to the glass surrounding the box.

"Unless Chase Kennedy can pull out some magic, Daddy's team very well might lose. But losing is a part of life, you know." Jessica looks over her shoulder, blond curls swinging as she smiles at me.

"No promises on that," I chime in. "I'm here as his 'good luck charm.'" I hold up air quotes. "But I'm pretty sure I'm failing miserably at my duties."

Frankie laughs. "Leo told me you went to all of Chase's high school and college games, and his dumb superstitious ass thinks you're the reason he's so good."

Jessica covers Asher's ears quickly. "Language!"

Frankie holds a hand to her mouth and giggles. "Whoops, sorry. But there aren't really a lot of other words that describe Chase Kennedy so well, besides…A-S-S." She turns to me with raised brows. "No offense, Whitney."

I chuckle. "No argument from me on that one."

Erica purses her lips and leans forward in her seat. "I'm just totally shocked Chase even has the humility to credit his wins to something other than his own almighty greatness and perfect arm that was placed on his body by God himself." She pushes an enormous pair of sunglasses onto her head and points at me. "That's quite the compliment to you, girly."

I rest my head in my hand and look back at the field, where the Riders just called their final timeout of the game. "Huh. I never thought of it that way. To be honest, I've never really thought the words *Chase* and *humility* could even go in the same sentence."

Frankie bounces her legs excitedly. "Ooh, Whitney! Tell us an embarrassing Chase story. My hubby just got completely taken down, and I need the pick-me-up."

Jessica narrows her eyes at us with a smile, sensing the need for this to be an adults-only conversation, and sends Asher to play with his train in the corner, out of earshot.

I take a final swig of the pink stuff in my cup and turn toward the other women. "Okay. When he was sixteen, this girl had a massive crush on him. Like a weak-in-the-knees, can't-speak-around-him kind of crush. It was sad, but sweet."

"Chase had groupies in high school? I'm so shocked," Jessica says with an eye roll.

"No kidding," I add. "Freaking Six…he's been drowning in them since kindergarten. But anyway, this particular girl got a little nervy one day and hyped herself up enough to ask Chase to be her homecoming date after school one day. She was probably quivering. And in true Kennedy fashion, he looks her right in the eyes and says, 'I'm already going with Chelsea and Britt.'"

Frankie almost chokes on her drink. "He had *two* homecoming dates?"

I shrug with a nod. "Both volleyball players. So the shy girl was *so* furious, she took her calculus textbook and smacked him with it. Right in the…" I eye Jessica to make sure Asher can't hear, but he's lost in his train world and can't hear a thing. "Balls. Just like, *wham*! In the crowded parking lot."

Erica gasps and laughs heartily. "He kinda deserved it."

"He totally did," I agree. "And I was putting my stuff in my car, getting ready to leave, watching this entire interaction. It was painful. When the girl walked away, I went over to Chase, and he was literally in tears. It was so hard not to laugh, but I let him hide in the back seat of my car and went to the school nurse to get him an ice pack. He'll deny crying to this day, but you heard it here first, ladies."

"That is rich." Frankie leans her head back and touches her necklace again. "He is a special one, that Kennedy. I'd love to see him through your eyes." She turns to me and shakes her head. "Knowing his whole history and all the freaky weird Chase stuff that probably goes through his mind all the time…"

Jessica nods. "You gotta wonder…how true are the rumors?" She lowers her voice to a tiny whisper and leans in close to us. "I mean, he's supposed to be some kind of absolute *god* in bed. Is it all talk?"

No, Jess. It's not.

Frankie narrows her eyes at me. "You two have really *never* done it? I mean, this is Chase we're talking about. Aren't you just dying of curiosity?"

I look out to the field and watch the team jog out of the huddle as the timeout ends. It's the Riders' ball, and Chase is running along the sideline, hyping up the crowd, and blowing kisses at screaming girls. "I guess I'm a little curious," I say, my voice small and quiet.

"Damn right you are!" Erica claps her hands. "If you ever do, you better tell us about it. And by it, I mean…" She uses her hands to make the shape of a dick between her legs. "*It.*"

I laugh. "Let's see if they can pull this game out."

I scoot forward in my seat and watch Chase closely. He's been running noticeably more hands-off plays this game to avoid long throws with that shoulder sprain. Which is smart, but without Chase's cannon throws and glory catches from Leo Sterling, the Riders' offense is looking a tad sorry.

He needs to throw a bomb if they're gonna have a chance at winning this game, or even tying it. He shouldn't throw a bomb. Frankly, his ass should be parked on the bench. But I know Chase way too well to even try to suggest that he sit for a game or two.

I squeeze my hands together and swallow hard as they line up on offense, and Clay flicks the ball to Chase.

Come on, Kennedy. Be smart. It's better to lose one game than injure yourself worse.

Of course, he can't hear my thoughts, and in the blink of an eye, he launches a Hail Mary pass that looks like it may be intended for Leo.

But that's not where it goes. The ball curves off to the side, severely lacking Chase's signature spiral and accuracy, lands right in the hands of the Broncos' defensive back, and he charges it down the field as the clock runs out.

"A pick?" Frankie says under her breath. "I can

barely remember Kennedy ever throwing a pick until this season. He really is off his game."

"Guess I'm just a terrible good luck charm." I force a laugh, but keep my eyes fixed on Six. He's in pain. It wasn't just a bad pass, it's his damn shoulder. And no one knows but me.

As the players' families start to file out of the seats and head down to the field, I know I have to talk to him. I can't let him keep making this sprain worse by trying to be Tom Brady all the time. Plus, if he hurt it even more with that throw, I should take a look at it as soon as possible.

"Well, ladies, it's a consolation-sex kinda night," Erica says loudly as she clicks down the stadium corridor in her spiky heels.

Jessica frantically covers Asher's ears just in time and shoots Erica a look.

Frankie snorts.

By the time we make it through the maze that is the Riders stadium and down to the field, most of the guys are heading to the locker room, surrounded by a palpable feeling of defeat.

Leo pulls his helmet off and shakes out his hair, kissing Frankie and pressing his forehead to hers.

Elliot picks up his son and swings him over his shoulder, squeezing Jessica tightly against them.

I scan the pack of grumbling, frustrated football players for Six. I know how much Chase hates to lose. Really, really hates it. I wish everyone else knew what I know. That the loss is entirely not his fault. He's *hurt* and way too proud to admit it.

I finally find his chiseled face, smeared with dirt and sweat. His eyes are low, and he's chewing on his mouth guard in a pissed-off but dangerously *sexy* way.

I push my hormones aside and watch him. He clutches his helmet at his side and doesn't so much as look at any of the media. His jaw is clenched, and his fists are tight.

I know now isn't the time to ask him about his shoulder, especially because he's so adamant about keeping it between us. So I stay on the side of the field by the tunnel and try to go as unnoticed as I can while all the other players trudge into the locker room. The wives and families dwindle, and the crowd empties from the stadium.

I'm not leaving until I talk to him.

The stadium is basically a ghost town now, with the occasional scurrying cameraperson or straggler fans. I lean against the concrete on the inside of the tunnel and check my phone.

One by one, the Riders walk out of the stadium. Some meet their wives in the garage. Others just hop into their noisy sports cars.

The minutes tick by, the players are all leaving, but…no Six.

I sink down and sit right on the pavement, throwing any bit of care about getting stains on my white jeans out the window.

Where the hell is he?

I hope he's not getting an earful from his coach about screwing up. Goddamn stubborn Chase.

Finally, I hear sneakers on the ground and jump up in anticipation. But the frame coming out of the locker room is definitely not Chase's. Lanky and quiet, Matt McKenzie gives me a smile as he walks by.

"You're Kennedy's friend, right? Waiting for your man?"

"Oh!" I brush off my pants. "He's not my man. But yes, I am his friend."

Matt keeps walking and shrugs, holding a duffel bag over his shoulder.

I peer down the tunnel and notice the air getting cooler as the sun starts to set. What is he gonna do, sleep in there? There's no way I missed him. Right?

"Nit Whit?"

A rush of relief and a flight of butterflies swirl through my chest. "There you are, Six."

"What the hell are you still doing here?" He cocks his head and smiles at me, and the dark note of defeat in his eyes visibly disappears.

"I—"

Before I can form another word, his arms are wrapped tightly around me, pulling me into his jersey and his scent and…him.

"I'm so happy to see you right now," he whispers.

My Chase. My closest friend who will never admit he needs anything except me.

I shut my eyes and take a deep breath, feeling him rest his chin on my head. I hug him back, and everything in my heart feels warm and happy and right. Like nothing else matters except for Chase's strong arms and broad shoulders and beating heart.

Because Chase is my *best friend.* And that's how best friend hugs make you feel.

Right?

seventeen

Chase

"It's your shoulder, isn't it?" Whitney reluctantly wiggles out of my embrace and gives me a sympathetic look.

"Shhh." I place two fingers over her mouth, trying not to notice how sexy and soft and *kissable* her lips are. "Keep your voice down, Whit." I glance around the tunnel outside the locker room. Thankfully, no one's around.

"Wow, someone's a *little* paranoid." She laughs softly.

I check down the corridor again, but there's no one in sight.

Whitney leans against the wall, bouncing up on her toes and giving me a knowing look. "You don't throw picks, Chase Kennedy."

"Damn right I don't," I mumble, inching closer to her and placing one hand on the concrete wall behind her, making the space between us almost disappear. "But that's what it looks like to everyone after that last pass."

Whitney looks up at me, and I lose myself in her wide, sparkling brown eyes and constellations of freckles dotting her nose and cheeks. "Everyone except me," she whispers.

"Yeah, Nit Whit." I can't even try to fight how magnetically I'm pulled to her right now. Of course she knows it wasn't a bad pass. Of course Whitney knows exactly what's wrong and probably how to fix it, because she's Whitney. Because she's had me figured out since preschool, and through everything, she's never stopped understanding me.

She nods slowly, clearly giving in to the palpable attraction almost as much as I am. Her cheeks are flushed, and her expression is one I've seen a million times, yet somehow entirely new.

Her back is flat against the wall, and I press both of my hands against the concrete, unable to resist holding my body against hers.

She quickly turns her head to peer down the hall, but there's nobody here except us. "You should… um…" Her voice is tiny and thin, and she keeps her gaze off to the side. "Rest your arm a bit."

She won't look back at me, because she knows that when she does, we'll both have to face whatever is burning and sparking and crackling between us. It's not friendship. And it's more than sex.

I don't know what it is. But every single molecule of my body is way too desperate to find out. I touch her face and turn her back toward me, holding her cheek and stroking it with my thumb. She looks at me, and she *sees* me. She's stood here for hours waiting for me.

"Chase—"

I press my lips to hers.

She gasps through the kiss, almost as confused and surprised by it as I am. But in seconds, she's kissing me back.

I hold her tight against the wall, cupping her soft, gorgeous face with my hand. She tastes bright and sweet and vibrant, like everything Whitney Cooper has always been.

Her curves arch and lean into me, and I press against her tightly. I'm not thinking with my dick. I'm not even thinking about banging her. Not right now.

This isn't a bang kiss. I don't know what this kiss is. It's not part of our sex game, and it sure as hell is not part of our friendship. But I couldn't physically look at her for another second and not be kissing her. It just wasn't an option.

Finally, common sense and reality crash over her, and she draws her mouth away from mine. "Six, what are you—"

"I don't know."

"This isn't part of the—"

"I know."

She draws in a slow breath, her chest rising and swelling against me.

It takes me a second to realize I'm still holding her face, and I slowly lower my hand and step back.

Her lips are still parted, and the expression in her eyes is every bit as freaked out as I am.

It occurs to me that maybe I should explain why I just kissed my best friend with a level of passion and intimacy that is completely foreign to me…and *completely* off-limits for us. "I just…" I run a hand through my hair and glance down the empty corridor.

"You waited here. And you know about the shoulder. And everything feels kinda…"

"Mixed up," she finishes, stepping away from the wall and pushing her hair behind her ears, clearly still a little rattled.

"Yeah." I nod and try to shake off the weird and confusing tension. I've never wanted to kiss Nit Whit before. I mean, I've thought about piping her plenty of times. But she's hot, and I'm a dude. So that's not that strange.

But I don't know what this is. Somehow, our sex lessons have blurred the lines between friendship and fucking and…romance?

No way. I don't do romance. I just got caught up in some weird-ass feeling because of the game and my arm and her…everything.

"You better get home, Six. I'm serious about the whole resting thing." She playfully bumps my side as we start walking out of the stadium toward the garage. "Stubborn ass."

"Yeah, yeah," I groan, welcoming the eased tension and quick subject change. "You took an Uber here, right? C'mon, I'll give you a ride back to Melody's place in the Lambo."

She waves her hands around and laughs sarcastically. "Ooh, what a thrill."

"Hey, you know how many—"

"Chicks would get absolutely *soaked* at the idea of taking a ride in my car?" She mocks me in her go-to douchebag voice.

I shove her lightly, and we both laugh. "Well? Do you? Because it's quite a number, Whit."

She rolls her eyes and stands next to the neon-green

car as I click a button on my keys, and the doors swing up. "I have work in the morning."

I slide into the driver's seat. "Yeah, I know. I'm taking you back to Melody's, right?"

She sits in the car and pulls her seat belt on, then turns to me. Her gaze locks on mine for an extra beat, and I wonder if she's thinking about that kiss. I sure as hell am.

Something in her eyes is…different. I've seen every emotion and expression in the Whitney Cooper handbook, but I don't know this one. She looks wild and fiery and…wow. Really fucking hot.

"Whit?" I ask, feeling a smile pull at my lips as I realize I couldn't look away right now if I wanted to.

"When can we do third down?"

I draw back with raised eyebrows and laugh. "Loving the eagerness, Whit, I really am."

She shrugs and turns to look out the front windshield. "I'm just looking out for the efficiency of my own education, Six."

It's completely dark, and the air in the car is hot, and I want to kiss her again. I want to kiss her everywhere. I want to show her *everything*. I want to watch those brown eyes widen and sparkle with every move I make.

"Come over after work tomorrow," I say slowly, unable to resist the urge to slide a hand up her sexy, toned thigh.

"Good," she asserts. "The clock is a-ticking."

I swallow hard, remembering that she's doing all of this with me only to impress some finance-cubicle dude. Then we're going to be friends again. *Just* friends. Six and Nit Whit, with no benefits.

No lessons. The way it's always been. The way it should be.

But now I'm sitting in my car, looking at her soft hair and adorable nose and deliciously flawless body, and I'm trying to figure out how the hell we spent more than two decades together without ever being more.

eighteen

Whitney

I brew another pot of coffee in the break room at the hospital as I sit down for lunch. I've been in a fog all day. A big, hazy, floaty, confused fog. I'm not used to feeling uneasy, especially not at work. When I'm at the hospital, nothing matters except the patients and their health and their lives.

But today, I can't seem to shoo the flock of butterflies swirling through my stomach, or shake the image of Chase kissing me against the wall at the stadium yesterday.

Maybe I've had a bit too much coffee.

He was being Chase Kennedy. Flirty and sexy and *always* getting what he wants. I just never thought what he wants would be…me.

I shut my eyes and sip the hot coffee, leaning against the counter and quieting the schoolgirl in my mind who thinks Chase Quarterback Kennedy might be *into* me.

"It's *Chase*, for Christ sake," I mumble.

"Are you okay, Whitney?" Sky, the cheery-eyed new nursing assistant, gives me a concerned look.

"Oh!" I swallow a slurp of coffee and wave my hand in the air. "I'm totally fine. Just trying to briefly escape food-poisoning lady in room twelve."

Sky snorts and flips her shiny blond ponytail. "Yeah, she's not having the best time. I can head in and check on her, if you want."

I laugh sympathetically. "The joys of nursing. Thanks, Sky."

She gives me a sweet smile and slips out the door, leaving me alone in the break room. I puff out a deep sigh and slump into a worn-out plush chair next to the window.

The sun is beating down on Florida as hard as ever, but something about today seems extra bright. The sky is like an endless blue blanket, and the greenery seems to decorate the entire landscape.

Suddenly, I feel my phone vibrating with an incoming call, and I curse the little flip my heart does when I think it might be Chase.

It's a number I don't recognize. Probably some scam or sales call. Still, I hate being rude to salespeople, so I answer.

"Is this Whitney Cooper?" The deep male voice on the other end of the line is vaguely familiar.

"Yes," I say slowly.

"It's Peter. Peter Chapman, from the party."

Oh my *God.*

Nerves jolt through me, and I hop up out of the chair, pacing around the break room like an anxious twelve-year-old. "Peter, hey! It's so great to hear from you. I didn't expect you to call until you got back from London."

"I know." He chuckles softly. "But I ended up getting talked into an international cellular data plan by my company, and I figured, you know, why wait?"

Maybe because I can't really think about you at the moment since I have tentative plans to go to "third down" with my NFL star best friend tonight.

"Yeah, totally!" Jesus. I sound like my cousin. I clear my throat. "How's London been?"

"Oh, you know. Meetings and spreadsheets and a constant stream of emails and phone calls about which I have little to no interest. The office here is nice, though. Right in the city. Have you ever been?"

"Oh, no." I pick at a chip in the paint on the wall. "I've never been out of the country. I wanted to study abroad, but they only offered nursing classes in Europe during the fall semester."

"So, why didn't you go during the fall semester?"

I stifle a surprised laugh. "Because that's football season. I was a Florida Gator, you may remember."

"I can't relate, sadly. People at Colgate could take football or leave it. But wow." He draws out the word. "Quite the loyal fan. I didn't take you as a sports guru, but I can dig it."

"I wouldn't say guru. It's just kind of the culture there. Plus, my best friend was the quarterback of the team, so it was a whole thing."

Peter makes a sort of choking sound. "Wait, *what*?"

I laugh nervously. "Chase Kennedy? He plays for the Riders now, so I see him all the time."

My mind flashes and races and jumps around. *Kiss. Wall. Hot tub. Kiss.*

I hold the windowsill and steady myself.

"Yeah, uh, I know who Chase Kennedy is. He's one of the best QB's in pro football." His tone sounds a bit concerned. "You didn't mention that at the party the other night." He forces something that sounds like a laugh.

Suddenly, I feel horribly awkward. Is there a reason I didn't bring Chase up when I met Peter? No. Why would there be?

"Oh." I flick my hand dismissively, even though he can't see me. "It's really not a big deal. We've been friends since we were *literally* in diapers. He's just Chase. Kind of a pain in my ass, honestly."

The tension over the phone seems to ease, although my gut is still tight. Why does it feel like I'm lying? Chase and I *are* just friends. That hasn't changed and never will.

Regardless of our plans for later.

"Huh. Well, you do seem to get more fascinating every minute of a conversation, don't you, Whitney?"

"That's what they tell me," I say jokingly. "So, are you doing any traveling while you're there? Or mostly staying in London?" I divert.

Peter muses about weekend trips to Prague and Venice, and I half listen while I adamantly remind myself that *he* is the reason I have this whole crazy agreement with Chase in the first place. I want *Peter*. I want to impress him and wow him and hopefully find forever with him.

With Peter, that is.

"That sounds incredible. I'm cooped up in the hospital for another several hours, but after that I'll be…" *Finding out what third down consists of.*

"Going for a run or something, probably. Nothing like traipsing around Europe, that's for sure."

"I'm honestly just ready for this trip to end. I'm really looking forward to our date." His voice is so steady and certain, with just the right hint of sweetness.

"Me, too!" I blurt a little too excitedly.

"Well, I'd better go. Heading into a meeting in five. It was wonderful to talk to you, Whitney Cooper."

"Yeah, same here. Have a good meeting," I say with a laugh, not really sure what you're supposed to say to someone before they do something that isn't emergency surgery or a football game.

I set the phone down on a table and slouch back into the soft chair.

I have to shake off all this weirdness about Chase. It's natural for things to get a little messy when you bring physical intimacy into a twenty-eight-year-old friendship. It gets even messier when that friend is an actual god of sex.

I *have* to keep it physical. No more butterflies, no more kisses—unless they're part of the plan.

I know it's nothing but a little fun for Chase. He likes teaching me, and I need to learn. And that's all there is to it.

nineteen

Chase

I take a long, deep breath and lean against the railing of my balcony, watching the last bit of sunlight disappear behind the Miami Beach skyline. The air is sticky and humid, and it settles like a warm blanket on my skin. I roll out my shoulder, noticing that the pain is starting to go away, or maybe I'm just distracted.

I feel my phone in my pocket vibrate with a text.

Nit Whit Cooper: *On my way, Six. Leave the door unlocked.*

I bite my lip and slump down onto the huge patio couch. I narrow my eyes and stare at the text for way too long.

The kiss in the stadium was just a moment. It was a one-time thing. The product of a shitty game and seeing my favorite person.

But I've never wanted to kiss Whitney before… unless…did I? I don't even fucking know anymore. All I know is I can't be in this weird-ass mood thinking about *feelings* when I'm supposed to teach her how to suck my dick.

I get a little hard at the thought and pick up my phone to text her back with just one word.

Balcony.

Staying out of the bedroom will keep things chill and purely physical and avoid any accidental kissing or, God forbid, *cuddling*.

I prop my feet on the coffee table in front of me and laugh to myself about the insanity of this whole situation. And about how hyped sixteen-year-old Chase would be if he knew one day he'd be sitting on his penthouse balcony waiting for Whitney Cooper to come over and give him head.

Shit, he'd be hyped just to know Whitney is still his best friend. I'm so fucking glad she's my best friend, and I'm beyond determined not to let this arrangement fuck it up.

"Look at you, so pensive." Whit's voice hits me like sweet, sexy music as she walks through the sliding doors and joins me on the sofa outside. "What's going through that deep, dark, terrifyingly dirty mind of yours?" She ruffles my hair playfully.

She's wearing tiny black shorts and an oversize Gators Football T-shirt that was probably mine at some point. She tucks her legs up underneath her, and I admire their perfectly toned and slender shape.

I think about touching them. Grabbing them. Having them wrapped around me.

"You know, the usual," I say.

"Football and sex?" she says with a laugh.

"Am I that simple?" I turn to her with a half smile.

"You're just…Six. You're who you've always been." She smiles brightly, and something in her expression is so comforting and familiar. It's the way

Whitney's always looked at me. Like she knows me inside and out. Like she can predict everything I think and feel and do.

It's not how she was looking at me at the stadium yesterday.

I decide quickly that she's clearly forgotten about that, or at least pushed it away, and I do the same.

"So…" I run my tongue across my bottom lip and angle my head down, giving her my token suggestive look. "Third down."

"Let me guess." She leans close to me and points a finger to her deliciously hot mouth. "It involves this."

"Wow." I wink and run my thumb along her lips. "Someone's been doing her homework."

She narrows her eyes, making them spark in the moonlight. "You didn't give me any homework."

"I didn't have to."

She smiles and looks out at the view, something that looks like hesitation flashing across her face. "I gotta be honest, Six. This one kinda scares me."

I instinctively push a strand of her silky hair behind her ear. "Understandable. I mean, we are dealing with—"

She holds up a hand and makes a face of disgust. "If your dick has a name, I do not want to know it."

I frown and stifle a laugh. "Okay, but seriously, what's the big deal with oral? I know you're not some kind of germ freak, considering *I* was the one who flipped shit when you wanted to play with a bowl of raw eggs in third grade. I mean, Whitney. Ew."

She snorts at the memory. "I'm an ER nurse, Chase. The human body doesn't intimidate me."

"Neither does salmonella, apparently," I add.

"It's just…Troy and I never really…" She makes a vague gesture that I assume means she barely ever went down on her boyfriend of six years.

I laugh and draw back in shock. "Define 'never really.'"

"Like, twice." She swallows and looks down, toying with a thread on the T-shirt. "Maybe three times. He said it wasn't his thing."

"Blow jobs? They're not his *thing*?"

She purses her lips and nods slowly.

I feel my jaw drop and shake my head. "Well…" I slide my hand around the back of her neck and turn her head so she's facing me, looking right into my eyes. "They're my thing."

Her eyes widen with that same eager curiosity I saw in the hot tub. An expression that can get my cock completely fired up in less than thirty seconds. "Show me, Six," she whispers.

Those soft, pink, needy lips don't have to tell me twice.

I kiss her hard, knowing full well *this* kiss is driven by sex and desire and the ache of physical attraction.

She kisses me back, perfectly matching my dirty, sexy energy.

I slide my tongue into her mouth as my hands pull her body onto my lap, and I can already feel heat and blood racing to my dick.

I slip my hands under her shirt and cup both her breasts, feeling her rock and arch against me. I yank the shirt off of her and kiss down her neck and chest.

She leans back and breathes rapidly, letting the moon bathe her in a soft white glow. Her chest rises and falls in my hands, and I draw in a sharp sigh as she gently strokes my hard-on.

My abs are tight, and everything feels hot and achy.

"Should I—" she whispers.

"Yes."

She slides off my lap and kneels on the floor of the balcony, looking up at me with parted, swollen lips. Lips that should have been around my cock a long-ass time ago.

"Here," I say softly, reaching for a pillow from the couch and tossing it down. "For your knees."

She scoots her legs onto it and laughs. "I never took you for such a gentleman, Six."

I shrug and run my hand through her hair, holding her delicate, freckled cheek. "See? I can still surprise you, Nit Whit."

She pulls lightly at the waistband of my sweatpants, staring up at me with those damn eyes. "Should I…"

"Yes." I smile at how adorable she is. I've never thought of a chick who's on her knees about to blow me as *adorable* before, but somehow it fits with her.

She pulls my pants and boxers off, and sparks jolt through me at the feeling of her touch on my skin.

She draws back at the sight of my raging erection. "Jesus, Six."

I laugh softly and run my fingers through her hair.

She tilts her head and closely examines my cock. "I mean…really?"

"Complimenting your teacher isn't going to get you an A, you know." I shoot her a wink, eyeing the burning space between her lips and my dick and wishing it would disappear.

She smiles and rolls her eyes, leaning forward a

tiny bit, moving her hands up my legs just slowly enough to send heat waves all the way down to my toes. "Where do I start?" She grazes the length of me with her fingertips, so light and gentle and teasing.

I jerk forward and feel my heart rate pick up. "You're a smart girl. Take a guess."

A smile pulls across her face, dirty and curious and hot as hell. She dips her chin down and softly runs her tongue along the tip of my dick, moving her hand up to grab the base of it.

I'm completely hard and hot and so fucking desperately turned on, but I know we need to take this one slow. We can take all damn night if she wants to. I just like watching her.

"There you go," I whisper, my voice sounding raspy and breathless.

I hold her head and lightly guide her as she slides her mouth around my dick and moves it down.

Her eyes spark with heat and fire and lust, and my whole body rocks and aches and responds to every tiny move she makes.

"Is that good?" she says quietly with that dirty-shy thing playing in her expression.

"Yeah." I choke a laugh, barely able to see straight with how turned on I am and how much I don't want her to stop. "It's fucking good."

She pulls away, and I gently guide her head back to my dick. "Rule number one: Don't stop doing that," I whisper.

Her eyes brighten, and I watch as a new kind of sexy confidence comes over her. It's a side of Whitney I've never seen before, and that in itself is a fucking crime.

She's having fun with it now, licking my shaft and tip, gliding her tongue and lips over every inch.

Blood and heat and an unbelievable tension surge in my cock, which just gets harder and bigger with every stroke of her mouth.

My abs are tight, and hot chills race down my spine as I lean forward into her.

"You don't…" I grip her hair with one hand and squeeze the couch cushion with the other, feeling my heart beating hard as fuck. "Need much help."

She slides her mouth up my dick and playfully licks the tip. "You're so hot, Six." Her words are breathless and desperate, consumed by desire and the fireworks of passion.

I never knew how badly I wanted to see her like this. To feel her like this. To hear her say those words and watch those enormous brown eyes glint in the moonlight and stare up at me with sinful lust.

I draw in a sharp breath as she pulls back and gives me a dirty smile, stroking my erection with her hand, holding it against the swell of her breasts.

The lights of the skyline are scattered in the distance, and the sticky fall air presses on me as my body gets hotter and tighter and needier every second.

"Any notes, Teacher?" She winks at me, obviously feeling how close I am and teasing me.

I don't mind a bit. I bite my lip and hold her chin, angling her face up to look at me. "You like this, don't you?"

She runs her lips along the length of my shaft, sending more waves of electricity through my body. "Shut up."

Her eyes say it all. She isn't the only one who can read her best friend like a fucking book. Whitney Cooper is awakening her most wild sexuality, right on this balcony, with her lips around my cock.

Heat and need continue to build as she sucks and licks and enjoys every second of it. I can feel my balls squeezing and my dick pulsing in her mouth.

Whitney knows I'm about to come and looks at me with wide, sparkly eyes.

Pleasure hits me like a fucking tsunami, crashing over my body as I release over and over again. My heart bangs in my chest, and a husky moan escapes from my throat.

Whitney draws back, a sexy smile on her face as she wipes her lip with her thumb.

I decide I've never seen anything hotter in my life.

Whit rests her chin on my leg, leaning into me and gazing at me with a look of pure satisfaction. "Third down." She grins.

"You're going straight to the Pro Bowl, Nit Whit. Now, your turn." I wink and playfully touch her mouth. "You wanna go into the bedroom? It might be easier for—"

She laughs and stands up, curling onto the couch next to me and looking out over the expansive view. "Six, I needed you to teach me how to do that. I think I'm okay on the receiving part."

Her expression flashes with hesitation and conflict, almost like me returning the favor of third down would make her feel something she's not ready for. Something she's scared of.

I remind myself of her boundaries and take a deep breath, pulling my sweatpants back on. I look at

Whitney, shaking my head. "The fact that you've been hiding these world-class blow-job skills is actually a crime against humanity."

She chuckles. "Honestly, I didn't know I could do it like…that. I don't know what came over me. Must have been your magical quarterback spell."

"That's never even fazed you before." I narrow my eyes and meet her gaze, realizing how desperately I want to kiss her. I think, for a second, she wants me to. Something burns between us, some strange mixture of sex and friendship, of passion and comfort.

Suddenly, she rolls her eyes and looks out over the balcony, forcing a laugh and shrugging, as if to push away the moment. "I've never had your dick in my mouth before, either, Six."

I laugh heartily and wrap my arm around her shoulders, still wanting to kiss her. "Talk about a crime against humanity."

She rests her head on my arm, and we watch Miami Beach sparkle and glow for miles.

I swallow hard, remembering that messing around with Whit is very temporary, and it's pretty much certain that I'll never see those fiery eyes looking up at me like that again. I'll never watch her experience passion and desire and *that* kind of fun again.

She clearly doesn't want to feel anything, and I just flat out don't know how.

I pull in a deep sigh, wondering how the hell "just friends" has ever been enough. How it ever will be after this.

twenty

Whitney

It was a blow job. It can't be emotional. I mean, even the most love-struck obsessive couples don't have *emotional* blow jobs. Do they? It's not a thing. It felt so intense only because I'm not used to it. And Chase is sinfully hot. And the fact that he was looking at me with something deeper than raw sex drive and physical desire was purely in my imagination.

Right?

"Cuz!" Melody snaps her fingers in my face. "Hello? I'm asking you if this is cute." She holds up a strappy blue crop top and jiggles the hanger.

"Sorry. I'm spacey. Just tired. But yeah, I like it! It's very you." I smile brightly and run my hand along the rack of shirts, trying to force last night off my mind.

I promised Melody a cousins' mall day since I don't have work and she doesn't teach yoga until seven p.m., but I can't seem to get myself into the shopping mood.

"Okay, Whit." She shoves the shirt back onto the rack and loops her arm through mine. "Let's go get a cup of coffee, and you can tell me what on earth is *really* going on."

I groan and let her drag me out of the store, knowing full well I'm an absolutely terrible liar, and since Melody already knows what's going on with Chase, I might as well just dump the rest of it on her.

"Two grande iced caramel macchiatos upside down with extra caramel and whipped cream, please!" Melody sings as we walk up to the Starbucks kiosk. "Trust me," she says sternly, catching a glimpse of my eye roll.

I snort. "As long as you're paying, girl, I'll drink your crazy liquid sugar all day."

She hands her card to the barista and arches a brow at me. "This coffee is a symbol of truth."

"What on earth are you talking about?"

"I'm buying you a coffee, right?"

"Right," I say slowly, nodding at the drink getting doused in whipped cream. "If you can even call it that."

"This is my gift to you, and in return you are going to tell me the truth and the *whole damn* truth. Because I know something's up with you. And I think I know who it's about. Got it?"

There's no point in denying anything. I take a deep breath, tearing the paper off a straw and popping it into the top of one of the drinks on the counter. "Okay, Mel."

We sit across from each other at a table next to the splashing fountain in the middle of the mall.

"Dish," she demands with a slurp of her caramel drink.

"It's about…Chase." I lower my voice and peek around, as if some random group of mall patrons is going to hear me and judge the messy pile of confusion that is my love life.

Melody fakes an exaggerated gasp. "Chase? What? I never would have guessed. Don't tell me you're running into problems with your little sex game."

I stifle a laugh and hush her. "Would you please keep your voice down? And don't say I told you so. Okay…" I sip the sweet drink that has the vague taste of coffee buried deep within it. "Here goes. I think I might have just a tiny, itty-bitty, *smidge* of a crush on Chase."

"I'm shocked," she says with flat sarcasm. "Keep talking."

"Last night, we had…oral sex."

"Ew! Why do you call it that? This isn't a clinic, Nurse Cooper."

"Fine." I lean close and meet her bright blue eyes. "I *blew* him. Better?"

Melody nods approvingly. "Details. Please, *God*, details."

"It was…" I toy with a hangnail on my thumb and try to find the words to describe that particular activity. There really aren't any that will do it justice. "Really something. I never thought of that part of sex as one of my favorites, but…" I can't fight the giddy smile that pulls at my lips. "I had so much fun. It was so hot and wild and like nothing I'd ever done before. Nothing I'd ever *felt* before."

"Nothing like a good beej, cuz."

"Can't argue with that. Apparently."

"So, from that it just seems like you guys are hooking up. Sounds physical enough to me." She shrugs.

"That's the thing. It was *so* insanely physical. But

sometimes, he would look at me, and it was, like, something more. It was hot and everything, but it was…Chase. I guess that must be what's freaking me out. I think it was so amazing only because it was with *him.* The way we know each other, the way we see each other… It was like all our years of friendship and constantly being there for each other somehow made it way more intense, as if our bodies and hearts have subconsciously wanted to explore each other for a decade. It was in his eyes. He has such incredible eyes—"

"Okay." Melody holds up her hand and cuts me off. "I'm not gonna say I told you so, even though, wow…I *literally* did." She rolls her eyes and nudges my arm playfully.

"I'm not falling for him, Mel. It's not like that. It's just that I'm seeing him in a new way, I guess." My voice trails off as I look into the rushing fountain and wonder what I would wish for if I threw a penny in it right now.

"Do you want to, like, be with him?" She twirls a strand of pink hair and narrows her gaze.

"It wouldn't matter even if I did. Chase Kennedy doesn't want to be with me. Or anyone. He doesn't know how. I'm sure he just thinks he got some nice head from his hot friend and nothing more."

She purses her lips. "You guys still have to go all the way, right?"

"Yeah." I nod. "But maybe I should cut it off. End the whole sex lesson thing before I get in too deep and feel something…serious. Not only is he a grade-A womanizer, he's my best friend in the world—both valid reasons why I can*not* fall for him."

"Oh hell no." Melody's eyes widen, and she shakes her head. "You can't cut it off, cuz. Then he'll know you're catching feels. And if he thinks you're getting all lovey-dovey and totally crushing out on him, that'll for sure mess with your friendship. He'll feel weird about the whole thing, and you don't want that. I know how important he is to you."

"Crap," I whisper. "You're right."

"You gotta finish out the agreement. At least just to prove it's purely physical and you still see him solely as just your hotshot douchebag best friend. He can't know you're feeling *anything* beyond friendship and a little bit of fun sex."

I drink my caramel thing and shut my eyes, nodding slowly.

"Besides." She lifts a shoulder and bites her lip. "Maybe if you bang him, this will go away. Like, get it out of your system or whatever. As long as you can keep it physical."

I swallow hard and think of all the years I've spent side by side with Chase Kennedy and how I've never so much as considered the idea of having a crush on him. These few short weeks won't matter in the long run. "I can keep it physical," I assert, trying to convince myself as much as my cousin.

"There you go. Just remind yourself: no emotions. It's Chase!" She flicks her hand. "Lovable asshole Chase, who's been your friend as long as I've been your cousin. Oh, and say it, please." She grins widely. "Just once."

I roll my eyes and chuckle. "You were right, Mel. You were *so* right."

She reaches across the table and gently holds my

hand, her tiny wrist tattooed with the word *Peace* and her slender fingers decorated with rings. "You'll be fine. And look at it this way!" She gives my hand a squeeze. "You said you felt…*wild.*"

I laugh. "Yeah."

"So, at the very least, your little plan is working, right?"

I smile and feel a sudden sense of relief. "Yeah, I suppose it is."

I just hope I'll be able to feel the same wildness when I'm looking at someone other than Six and his dirty-blond hair and magical, soul-melting eyes.

twenty-one

Chase

"Good practice, everyone." Coach Watson's voice booms through the locker room. "Rest up for Sunday."

I sit on the bench in front of my locker and start unlacing my cleats. I subtly roll out my shoulder, thanking God it hurts a lot less today. Whit's electrifying blow job must have relieved more than just the tension in my dick.

The image of her wide eyes and naughty mouth must have raced through my mind a hundred times during practice. I have no clue why I can't stop thinking about it, but I'm chalking it up to the fact that it's Whitney, and the other night was just another level of satisfaction for some subconscious curiosity left over from high school or whatever.

No matter how many times I tell myself it's just physical, it's just *Nit Whit*, the whole thing makes me feel uneasy. I get this strange floaty feeling in my chest when I think about her now, and it's not me being horny and wanting to screw her. It's different. It's weird.

"Dude." I hear Elliot Danes' voice from a few feet away. "You're gonna have to ask Kennedy. Sterling's been out of the hookup game for a while now, and I was never really in it to begin with."

I see Matt McKenzie standing next to Elliot and Leo, clearly with some burning need for advice. Of course he asks Danes, aka Daddy Does No Wrong.

"He's right," Leo agrees, glancing in my direction. "This is a Chase Kennedy specialty. And trust me, I don't generally send anyone his way for this kind of advice."

"I can hear you, dickhead," I call in their direction. "Whatcha need, shrimp?"

Matt walks over and squats down on the bench next to me. "I'm looking for some lady advice."

I give him a cocky smile. "And you ask those pussies? Dude. They're both *married.* Two living, breathing examples of how to get your balls locked up in some chick's panty drawer."

For the first time probably ever, I don't *really* believe what's coming out of my incredibly douchey mouth.

"Yeah," Matt says through a laugh. "You're right, man. I am only twenty-three. You were probably a total player at my age."

I hold up a hand. "Okay, rule number one is that you have to stop acting like I'm your fucking dad. I'm still a player."

Yeah. A player who can't stop thinking about his childhood best friend and her freckles and shiny hair and cute-ass little nose.

"Right, true." Matt clasps his hands together. "So there's this girl. And she's giving me, like, hella mixed signals. It's confusing. I really want to get with her, but I don't want to do anything wrong."

I furrow my brow and shake my head. "Dude. You don't need mixed signals. You're an NFL QB." I pat his back, surprised at how nice I'm being to the rookie who poses the biggest threat my professional career has seen.

"Backup QB," he corrects with a humble smile that *almost* makes me like him.

"That was implied. Point is, you're past the time where you need to play mind games with women. You're a pro now, Junior. They're gonna start falling at your feet."

He shrugs and raises his brows. "I've never been much of a playboy."

"Lucky for you, I've been enough of one for everyone on this damn team. So I know what the hell I'm doing. Tell you what, meet us at the Atlantic tonight. I'll show you some classic ways to have a banging single life. So to speak."

Matt smiles and stands up. "Passing the torch, hell yeah. Thanks, Kennedy, that sounds sick."

"Yeah, don't say sick. And I'm not passing anything." I roll my eyes. "Whatever. Just be there at nine."

I decide tonight is as good a night as any for Whitney and me to score our…touchdown, since it's always been part of the deal, and I can't seem to stop picturing it. Besides, I can't get Junior laid and go home by myself.

Not when Whitney Cooper exists.

Matt walks back to his locker, and I toy with the idea of "passing the torch." Why does it sound like my era of being a fuckboy athlete drowning in pussy is over? Why does it feel like that? Why am I weirdly kind of a little bit *okay* with it?

Goddamn Nit Whit and her seductive mouth and enchanting eyes and personality that I've adored since I could walk. She gives me shit for casting a spell on everyone I meet, but she's the one who's really magic.

twenty-two

Whitney

"You can just drop me off in front," I say brightly to my Uber driver. "Thank you!"

The car pulls up in front of the glitzy skyscraper on top of which the Atlantic sits and overlooks downtown, filled with hotshots and money and fancy drinks.

I step out, and the car whips away from the building. The warm nighttime air wraps me up as I try to push away the swirl of emotions that races through my chest and heart and mind.

I pick up my phone and reread Chase's text, as if I wasn't staring at it the entire ride to the bar.

Meet me at The Atlantic. Take an Uber, because you're coming home with me. Touchdown awaits.

I silently curse the girly smile that pulls at my lips and the butterflies that soar in my stomach every time I read that stupid message.

It's just sleeping together. It's just Chase. It's part of the deal, a part I've known was coming from the very day I decided to take sex classes from my professional athlete best friend.

I'm still trying to figure out if that was a miserable lapse in judgment or the best thing I've ever done. My logical mind and lady bits can't seem to agree, and I refuse to let my heart enter the equation.

I step forward, and the sliding doors into the lobby open automatically. The cool AC blasts my skin, and I feel the prickle of goose bumps ripple down my spine as I walk into the elevator. Which is because of the icy air conditioning. It has nothing to do with seeing Chase and kissing Chase and banging Chase.

"Physical. Nothing more," I whisper during the blissfully private elevator ride. "Just sex. Have fun. Learn a thing or two. Don't fall for…"

The elevator slows to a stop as the doors glide open, and those goddamn brown eyes are already sparkling in front of me.

"There you are, Nit Whit." Chase's face is vibrant and bright. He's full of his usual Kennedy charm and charisma, but tonight he's more handsome than I've ever noticed, and just his smile is making my knees weak.

Stay strong, Cooper.

"Ask and you shall receive, apparently," I tease with an eye roll, careful not to let my gaze linger on the painfully tempting bulge in his khakis.

"Already got your favorite." He hands me a cold bottle of Bud Light and places his hand on my back, guiding me to the table where the other guys are sitting.

His hand slides lower and down my back, and I try to hide my gasp as he gives my ass a sneaky grab, an obvious reminder of what's happening later tonight.

As if I could have *forgotten.*

"Kennedy's best friend!" Frankie hops out of her seat and gives me a tight hug. She turns to Chase with her arm wrapped around me. "We completely love her, by the way." She looks back at me, her stunning green eyes bursting with joy.

Is that what people who are in love are supposed to look like?

"No offense, but I'm so glad you broke up with your lame-o boyfriend, because now you're at all the games and at the bars, and you're so fun!" Frankie flips a shiny lock of hair over her shoulder.

I laugh heartily and slide into the seat next to her. "Yeah, I'm so happy I get to see Six and his team and all you guys so much more now."

Jessica leans close to me. "It was very confusing to me at first that you guys are actually just friends and nothing more, because, I mean…" She nods toward Chase. "He puts his dick in everything that moves."

The joke stabs my chest way harder than I expect it to. I force a laugh and take a swig of beer.

I feel Chase's massive hands on my shoulders and lean my head back to look at him. "Hi, Six," I say with a laugh.

"Come here. Meet the little twerp who's trying to take my spot."

I stand up and chuckle in surprise. "You invited Matt McKenzie to come out with you guys?"

"Yeah, don't read into it. It's charity work. Like a Make-A-Wish kinda thing."

I snort and smack him lightly as we walk over to where Matt is standing by the roof railing.

Matt McKenzie is young, but definitely handsome. He doesn't have Six's palpable aura of arrogance—at least not yet—but he's got a lot of potential. And he's apparently a massive threat as quarterback, so this kid could definitely end up like Chase in a couple of years.

Although Chase was *never* shy or humble. He came out of the womb with a cheerleader's panties in one hand and an All-Star trophy in the other.

"Hey, I'm Matt. I saw you after the game the other day, but I don't think we've officially met." He holds out his hand and gives me a charming smile.

"Yeah, I heard you're the new QB with a better arm and a way more tolerable personality." I shake Matt's hand and wink at Chase.

Matt laughs softly and juts his chin toward Chase. "Nah, Kennedy's awesome. He's actually been helping me get into the Riders offense a lot."

"Is that so?" I narrow my eyes at Chase, who bites his lip and looks skyward. "He is quite the altruist. Always thinking of others."

"You're not officially my teammate until you and Whitney Cooper gang up on me." He gives Matt's lean shoulder a firm pat. "Congrats, bitch."

Matt and I laugh, and the three of us walk back to the table. I can smell Chase's cologne, and I can feel his rock of a tricep brushing my arm. I want to hold and touch and taste every last inch of him. I telepathically beg him to grab my ass again.

I slip back onto the barstool between Frankie and Chase, trying desperately to shake off my melty attraction and convince myself that it's all just hormones and sex drive and has nothing to do with the fact that I've always had an enormous soft spot for my endearing asshole of a best friend.

"*Chase Kennedy*, as I live and breathe," a deep, sensual woman's voice coos slowly.

High heels click on the rooftop as a tall, lean figure floats up to the table. Shiny, stick-straight black hair frames a face that is so beautiful it almost hurts to look at it.

"Is that Arabella Addams?" Frankie whispers.

"Holy shit, it is," Elliot responds with a chuckle from across the table.

The world-famous movie star is even more striking in person than she is in her series of action thrillers, where she plays a smoking-hot badass FBI agent and runs around chasing bad guys in Louboutins. Naturally.

"Damn. Go, Kennedy," Jessica says with a lift of her shoulder. She turns to Elliot and nudges his arm. "Babe! It's almost ten. Can you text the babysitter and make sure Ash goes to bed soon?"

They're all happy and cute with their kid at home, and Frankie and Leo are *literally* radiating love and perfection.

I swirl my beer and watch the string bean of a woman run her pointy fingers along Chase's arm, wondering how I—who's longed for love and commitment and forever since high school—ended up as the only single person at a table full of rich, hot NFL players and their equally hot wives.

"It's been, what, two years? *Way* too long." The actress' sharp blue eyes are practically undressing him right in front of us.

I swallow hard and feel my gut tighten. Would Six bail on our stupid little playdate to bang this tall drink of movie star water?

Of course he would.

He's Chase freaking Kennedy, and she's Aphrodite or whatever, and I'm just his childhood best friend. Who could blame him?

They've stepped away from the table, and I can't hear their conversation, but she's touchier than a kid at a petting zoo, and together they make a disgustingly sexy pair of famous people.

Just as I finish my beer, wrestling with the sinking feeling in the pit of my stomach, and accept the way tonight is going to turn out, Chase walks away from her.

He holds up a finger, and I can make out that he tells her to "Wait one sec," and hurries back over to the table.

Flashing me a classic Six grin that simultaneously makes my heart flip and my panties a little wet, he grabs Matt McKenzie's shoulder and drags him over to Arabella.

"Chase Kennedy doing God's wingman work. No fucking way," Leo says, shaking his head in disbelief.

Jessica leans forward and gasps through a laugh, blond curls falling all over her pretty face. "He's introducing her to the rookie." Her voice heightens with surprise.

"Is our little douchebag finally growing up? It's unthinkable," Elliot adds.

I don't even try to fight the wave of excitement that ribbons through me at the idea of Chase turning down a world-class hookup with the obviously interested Arabella Addams.

For me?

Matt and Arabella start chatting, and Chase turns away, sliding back onto the seat next to me.

The table is oddly silent for an extra beat, almost as if no one can comprehend a version of Chase Kennedy who makes a move like that.

"All right, I'll say it." Leo sets his glass on the table and narrows his eyes at Chase. "Who are you, and what did you do with our quarterback?"

"Ha-ha." Chase leans back in his seat and shrugs. "She gets around a lot, Arabella Addams."

"And?" Leo asks.

"Yeah…" Elliot eyes Chase. "When has that *ever* stopped you?"

"It's not that." Chase shakes his head.

Oh shit. Is he about to tell them that we have plans for a platonic sex lesson tonight? I stop breathing for a second.

"I've just heard she's a terrible lay," he says matter-of-factly with a sip of his beer.

Relief floods me as the guys laugh and roll their eyes and take Chase's obvious cue to stop the questioning.

His leg is pressing against mine underneath the table, and it doesn't have to be. There's plenty of room. I don't pull away.

I feel ten times more attracted to Chase every second, and watching him say no to a Hollywood beauty icon really tugged at my heart strings.

I slip my hand into the back pocket of my jeans and pull my phone out. I open up the Notes app and type something to subtly show Chase so I don't have to say it out loud.

Is that true? That's really why you pushed away Arabella Addams?

I nudge his thigh and hand the phone to him, keeping the exchange hidden underneath the table.

Chase glances down and reads the question, laughing softly. He turns his head to face me, his gaze smoldering and his lips just a few desperate inches from mine. "No, Nit Whit. It's not true." His voice is low and raspy and borders on a whisper.

I feel my heart skip a beat. "Six…" I frown and give him a look of confusion, consciously reminding myself to keep everything friendly and playful and simply platonic, just as it would have been before we started messing around in hot tubs and on balconies.

He shrugs and faces forward, finishing his beer. "I have plans tonight." The words slip out only loud enough for me to hear them, and a sexy, cocky smile plays at the corners of his mouth.

I stare down into my lap while I attempt to gain control of the obvious grin spreading widely on my face and the soaring feeling in my chest.

Suddenly, as I'm repeating over and over in my head Melody's warnings about keeping things physical, I hear the tapping of silverware on a glass, as if someone's about to make a toast or something.

The conversation at our table dies down as Frankie and Leo stand up. They keep looking at each other like giddy middle schoolers, their eyes sparking with passion and love and their smiles both equally radiant.

"So, guys…" Frankie sets her glass down, and I notice it's filled with water. "We want you all to be the first to know…" She looks adoringly at her devilishly handsome husband.

"There's a little Sterling on the way!" Leo blurts out, wrapping his arms around his wife and kissing her with a visible overflow of affection.

Frankie bubbles with laughter, and now I understand the vibrant glow.

Elliot and Jessica jump out of their seats and rush over to hug Leo and Frankie. "Hell yes! More parents on the team!" they exclaim though excitement and laughter.

I hug Frankie. "You two are gonna have the most beautiful and football-obsessed child the world has ever seen," I say.

Chase stands up and bro-hugs Leo. "A family man now." He pats his shoulder hard. "You've come a long way, Sterling."

Leo nods toward Arabella the actress, who's completely engaged in what appears to be a *fascinating* conversation with Matt McKenzie. "So have you, my man."

Chase affectionately puts an arm around Leo and the other around Elliot. "Now there's three daddies in the group."

Elliot groans.

"I take that back." Leo ruffles Chase's hair. "You'll never get to this point. Chase Kennedy will be getting new ass every weekend well into his eighties."

Chase's smile fades slowly, and his gaze meets mine. His expression fills with something new. A longing in his eyes I've never seen.

I furrow my brow and tilt my head, able to tell in less than a second that something is bothering him, although it's impossible to know what it is.

His face looks tender, and suddenly I see a flash of the six-year-old boy who fell off his bike. The eight-year-old boy who had to say goodbye to his beloved golden retriever. The thirteen-year-old boy who watched his mom pull out of the driveway with a suitcase and never come back.

I don't know how I'm supposed to keep it purely physical and fun tonight when every fiber of my body knows that he needs me as way more than a fuck buddy.

I've always been there for Chase, and that will never change. I just have to remind myself that my feelings of affection for him are out of friendship, and everything else is separate. And temporary.

So *dreadfully* temporary.

twenty-three

Chase

"I gotta say…" I nudge Whitney's side playfully as we walk into my apartment. "I've never had to lay two decades of groundwork for a slam."

I force myself to think about the fun, sexy, sinfully dirty game of student-teacher that I'm supposed to play with my best friend tonight. But I can't shake that damn nagging feeling in the back of my mind. It's been bugging me since Frankie told everyone she's got a little Leo bun in the oven and those guys said I'll never get to that point.

Because I don't *want* to get to that point. Ever. I'm Chase Motherfucking Kennedy. I slay pussy, and I kick ass, and I have no intentions of tying myself down.

When I was thirteen, I learned firsthand that marriage isn't real. Commitment never lasts. There's no such thing as "true love."

But why do they look so goddamn happy? Why does fooling around with Whitney have me questioning my entire existence? Why do I keep looking at her and thinking about her freckles on a tiny baby Chase?

"I'm not a *slam*, asshole." Her voice brings me back to reality.

I shoot her a wink and decide to shake off my feely bullshit once and for all. "I don't think you're ready, Nit Whit. I really don't."

I walk over to her and slide my hands around her waist, savoring every soft slope as her body leans into mine.

She looks up at me with the most eager eyes I've ever seen. "I'm ready, Six."

I didn't know how badly I needed to hear those words come out of Whitney Cooper's mouth.

Heat surges to my dick as I move my hands down her body and cup her perfectly round ass. I lean down and pick her up effortlessly. She weighs, like, nothing.

Whit giggles and wraps her legs around me tightly as I carry her into the bedroom and drop playfully onto the California king and its silky sex sheets.

I shift on top of Whitney and kiss her, once again cursing the stupid fucking thoughts that have been burning in my head since we left the Atlantic.

I'm finally about to screw my painfully hot best friend, satisfying every last drop of teenage curiosity and years of silent attraction.

But for some reason, I can't push away these damn feelings about Frankie and Leo and my mom and fucked-up nagging bullshit.

I would normally talk to Whitney about anything that bothers me. But now Whitney's underneath me in my bed, and I so desperately want to bang her, but I also really need my best friend.

"Six…" She pulls her lips off of mine and wiggles

out from underneath me. "You wanna tell me what's going on?"

Okay, *how the fuck* does she know? I'm making out with her. I'm hard as a rock—and I know she can feel it—but there she is. Being Whitney. With her brown eyes and her freckles and her uncanny ability to know what's on my mind before I even do.

I run a hand through my hair, giving her a quizzical look and trying hard to play it off. "What's going on is that your clothes are still on, and I don't know how your dumbass ex did things, but for me they come off." I lean over and touch her lips softly. "That's a pretty basic thing, but I guess we're really starting from scratch here, aren't we?"

"What's truly amazing, Kennedy…" She sits up on the bed and tucks her legs underneath her. "Is that after twenty-eight years of inseparably close friendship, you haven't accepted that I can just about read your mind."

I breathe out a deep sigh and sit up to meet her eyes. Her soft, kind, understanding eyes that I've looked to for comfort since I was a kid. Our sex game hasn't changed that, and I feel pretty relieved that it clearly hasn't changed the way she looks at me. The way she feels about me.

Everything between us just feels stronger, brighter, louder…friendship tangled up with passion and sex. I gotta say, I'm kind of digging it.

"I don't know, Whit. The guys just giving me shit tonight, I guess."

She gives me a *get real* look. "Come on, Six. The guys rip on you twenty-four hours a day. You *live* for the attention."

I half smile and reach for her hand without thinking. "That's true. But, you know, all that crap about me never having…" I wave my hand, finding these thoughts particularly unpleasant to say out loud. "That Leo and Frankie…whatever."

She narrows her eyes and laces her fingers through mine so gently I could keep her hand there forever. "A baby?"

"No. Well, yeah. I don't know."

Whitney has always been the easiest person in the world for me to talk to, but these words catch and stick in my throat. I want her to know what I'm thinking and feeling, but how can I express it when I don't even understand it myself?

"Let's say it together," she says softly, scooting forward and giving my hand a squeeze with both of hers. "Com-mit-ment."

I roll my eyes and chuckle. "I've never wanted anything like that before. I never will. But then I see Leo and Elliot, and it's like…fuck. It makes me feel…" I clench my jaw and dig for the word, focusing on the warmth in Whitney's gaze, admitting silently that her brown eyes feel like home. "Empty, I guess."

Those eyes sparkle with something vibrant for a split second, and she bites her lip, looking away quickly and then back at me. "People can change. Maybe you actually want something you didn't think you ever would." Her voice rises with a note of enthusiasm.

"Like what?"

"Like love. Forever. A family. Something that has more depth and meaning than one-night stands."

I shut my eyes and hold my breath, seeing flashbacks of my mom's Volvo whipping out of the driveway that rainy Tuesday morning fifteen years ago. My dad's words echo in my head over and over again: *Love isn't real, Chase. Just have fun while you can.*

"No, Whit." My voice sounds more stern than I intended. "I don't want any of that. Maybe that kinda shit works for you, and Sterling, and Danes. But not me." I hold up air quotes. "'Love' isn't in my DNA."

"You think that because of the divorce? Is that why you're…" She gestures vaguely up and down my body. "You? You're not just a douchey playboy—"

"Yes, I am. That's exactly what I am."

"No." She leans back and shakes her head slowly, looking at me like she's peeling back a layer she hasn't seen before.

I can't decide if I like it.

"Your parents' divorce ruined your faith in love. You don't think you're capable of it. It's why you scoff at the concept of a relationship and don't let anyone close enough to make you feel anything."

Except you, Whitney. And that's fucking terrifying.

I nudge her playfully, really wanting to get away from this heavy conversation. "Don't psychoanalyze me, Freud."

"I don't have to, Six. Whose house did you go to every day after school for two months because you couldn't bear to go home, knowing your mom wouldn't be there? Who made you mac and cheese and watched *Star Wars* a thousand times because it made you forget about everything? I was *there*, Chase. I lived it with you. I just didn't realize the impact it had."

I feel like my heart is beating too fast. "It's not like

that, Nit Whit. I don't screw around with women because I have some crippling emotional baggage. I'm the way I am because I'm an NFL quarterback. Please." I sound like I'm trying to convince myself more than her. She can tell.

Because it doesn't matter what I say or how persuasive I am. Whitney Cooper reads me like a fucking chapter book and understands me more than I've ever understood myself.

"Six." Her voice is thick with empathy, every ounce of her exuding tangible love. In a friend way, of course. Best friend love. Like always.

"You don't trust women not to leave. You don't trust anyone," she whispers slowly.

"I trust you," I say without hesitating or thinking.

We're pulled to each other like magnets now, our lips just inches apart, her chest rising and falling as her eyes glimmer with emotion.

"Why?" she asks.

"Because…" I lean close, feeling warm from the energy and beauty radiating from her. "Like you said. You were there. You've always been there."

I don't know if it's the fact that we're supposed to have sex tonight, or the way she sees me as so much more than just a fuckboy athlete, or maybe the realization that Whitney has never left my life and never will, but I have to kiss her. Again.

So I do.

She leans in and kisses me back, pressing passion and heat and electric sparks from her mouth to mine.

The kiss is slow and hard and heavy, and I feel the depth of our relationship sealing our lips with a kind of fire I've never felt before.

I guide her lips open with mine, sliding my hand onto her cheek, holding tightly her beautiful and delicate face while I taste the sweet sunshine of her on my tongue.

The pace picks up as we start making out harder and faster and deeper, our hands recklessly exploring each other as if there's not enough time in the night to touch everything we want to.

Her body arches into mine, her flawless tits desperate for me. Somehow, we ended up lying down again.

Blood courses through me and rages in my dick, and suddenly every muscle in my body is hot and tight and fucking begging for her. I want her right now more than I've ever wanted anyone or anything. I want her a thousand times.

"Six," she moans into my mouth, anxiously ripping at my T-shirt as I shift my body on top of hers.

"Nit Whit," I whisper back, biting her bottom lip softly as she pulls off my shirt.

We frantically tear off each other's clothes until we're both completely naked, twisted up with each other, consumed by nothing but aching desperation and sizzling need.

I grab her hips hard, kissing her neck and getting harder with every sinful moan and plea that leaves her mouth.

I slide my tongue down her chest and suck on her hard nipple as she breathes rapidly and writhes with arousal underneath my body.

I sit up and take a breath, barely able to control the hottest lust I've ever felt. I look into her eyes—they're enormous and bright. I can't wait to watch her experience this. To feel her.

She runs her tongue along her bottom lip and slips her fingers delicately onto my cock, fire burning in her gaze. “Teach me something, Kennedy.”

I jut my chin at her. “I’ll teach you everything.”

The room is practically dark, but I can see every inch of her silky skin and delicious curves. Her back arches against the bed, and her soft pink lips quiver with need.

Whitney. My Whitney.

I’ve been around the block with supermodels and movie stars, but I’ve never in my life seen someone as beautiful as who’s in front of me right now.

twenty-four

Whitney

I don't think I'll ever get used to Chase's absolutely perfect specimen of a dick. And I sure as hell won't get used to him saying things that sound like he might be rethinking his entire "no feelings" life philosophy.

I try to push away the tiny glimmer of excitement that sparked in my mind at the possibility of him wanting love. He'll never change. I adamantly remind myself of this over and over again now, in his bed, naked, soaking wet and desperate for him in a way I didn't even know was possible.

My heart races with every touch against his skin. His muscles are cut like diamonds, and I don't hold back in exploring every trace. I'm so overwhelmed by how sexy he is, my body aches and burns, and I feel like nothing could ever possibly satisfy the hunger in me.

Chase kisses down my stomach softly, grazing my quivering thighs with his thumbs and setting off a spiral of chills that goes down to my toes.

I shut my eyes and lean my head back, pressed with the weight of arousal and trying desperately to figure out how to keep my feelings strictly physical when tonight started the way it did.

I don't know how to take the emotion out of what Chase and I are doing now. I don't know if I can. I don't know if I want to.

I have to. No feelings, Cooper.

I look down at his mess of dirty-blond hair as he kisses and licks and sucks on every inch of me, savoring me like a sweet piece of candy.

I slip my fingers into his hair, gripping tight as he runs his tongue along the inside of my thigh, making me shake and gasp. His jawline is sharp and hot, and I watch it move across my body like it's meant to be there.

"So…" he rasps. "The thing about a touchdown…" He holds my hips and rocks them toward him. "Is that you have to get all four downs first."

I manage a sarcastic laugh through my breathless panting. "That's not even how football works, quarterback."

"Don't talk back to your teacher," he says in a playful tone.

The dominance and command in his eyes, mixed with the endearing sweetness of his warm smile, make without a doubt the sexiest cocktail of a man I've ever seen.

"We already did the kissing." He shifts my body underneath his chin. "Which you're getting pretty good at."

I giggle and lean into him, savoring every teasing, tickling moment of his mouth on me.

"Second down." He slips two fingers into my dripping center, making me squirm and moan and grip with pleasure.

I clutch the sheets and draw in a sharp breath, letting the hot pleasure of Chase's touch inside me ripple down my spine.

He looks up at me with an aching hunger shining in his brown eyes, his soft smile so sweet and sexy and…*Chase*. Butterflies soar through my chest, and I can't take my eyes off him. He's so unbelievably perfect, and I'm suddenly overwhelmed by the feeling that this should have happened a long-ass time ago.

"Third down. Now it's *my* turn, Nit Whit." He gives me a teasing wink, which only intensifies the waterfall between my legs.

"I feel like I'm about to live every girl's fantasy," I say breathlessly, sliding my hand through his sexy, messy hair as I try to take a mental picture of Chase Kennedy about to go down on me.

"And I'm about to live my own."

My body melts as he slides his tongue over me, teasing the insides of my thighs and inching closer and closer to the achy, needy, desperate part of me. My thighs are quivering, and my breathing is rapid. The only thing I can think about or feel is Chase. He's the only thing that matters or exists right now.

His lips graze my clit, making me shudder and gasp. He starts slow, kissing and licking me in a way that makes me feel like I've somehow never experienced *real* pleasure until this moment. Right now. With my best friend.

He moves his tongue on every perfect spot I didn't even know existed, and my heart slams in my chest, heat pools between my legs, and the room around me twists into a blurry, fuzzy dream.

Chase knows what he's doing, and he fucking loves doing it, which only makes me more turned on. His eyes spark with lust and attraction and hot need as he licks and kisses me, sending spirals of chills down to my toes.

The whole world seems to stop. There's no sound or sight or anything but Chase and his tongue and his eyes and his hands gripping my ass and hips.

He smiles sinfully, feeling me about to come, rocking my hips into his mouth as I shut my eyes and desperately moan his name. His magical name.

My muscles tighten and pull, and my whole body turns to liquid as fireworks explode against Chase, and release crashes over me like a tidal wave.

I feel shaky and hazy as I look down at him. At the perfectly chiseled jawline resting on my thigh. At the way he admires me and wants me and somehow sees me as the most familiar person on the planet and also a total mystery. Knotted and twisted and tangled up in each other, he doesn't know what we are, but I think he likes it.

I sure as hell do.

"Okay, Six." I finally catch my breath, still dizzy from pleasure. "So *that's* the magic."

He smiles and kisses his way up my body, savoring every inch and making me feel like a truly fine and precious thing. "That magic is only for you, Whit."

His lips find mine, and I shut my eyes tightly, forcing myself to remember it's just physical. We're having fun and learning and…exploring.

I feel his erection throbbing against me, and

suddenly my body is on fire for more. His cut muscles bulge and tighten, and everything about him is radiating sexuality.

He positions himself on top of me, and the sizzling touch of his skin all over me sends ripples of need through me.

"Fourth and goal?" I whisper with a smile as he kisses my neck and slowly spreads my shaking legs open. "Is that what it's called?"

He gives me a cocky smile, his gaze dripping with lust and desire and his rock of a body pressing against me, making me beg for more. "Yeah, Whit. Look at you with the football knowledge."

I give in to the urge to press my mouth to his as my hands eagerly explore the solid ridges of his back and shoulders. Neither of us can catch our breath. We're both completely consumed by the need to give our bodies what they're screaming for.

But Chase, who is apparently the master of teasing and self-control and waiting until I have to physically beg him to screw me, rocks against me slowly, making sure I'm so wet and tight and desperate I can't freaking see straight.

He shifts his rock-hard dick so it's barely touching my center, which is knotted and aching to be his home.

He reaches to the nightstand and grabs a condom, tearing it open with his teeth and rolling it onto his impressive length.

"Chase," I rasp, grabbing his hair and looking at him with a fierce, desperate fire of need blistering in my body and undoubtedly showing on my face. "Touchdown. Please."

"Hey." He grazes my lip with his thumb. "Who's the teacher here?"

I groan and laugh and yank his hair, squirming underneath him. "You're the worst, Six."

He runs his hands up and down my sides, stopping at my breasts to cup them and massage them and get me even more aroused, which I didn't even think was possible at this point.

"I want you so bad," I whisper, my head rolling back into the pillows, and my nails digging into his lower back, aching for him to fill me as hard as he can.

He fixes his gaze intently on mine, and for a second I'm surprised. I never pegged Chase as one for eye contact in bed, but in this moment, it would be a sin for either of us to look away.

All at once, he enters me, and I clutch him tight, feeling the complete size of him inside me, totally taking my breath away.

He thrusts in and out slowly at first, and pleasure registers on his face.

"Fuck, Whit," he whispers breathlessly. His hands move effortlessly all over my body as he drives his cock harder and faster.

I'm practically seeing stars, my body wrapped around him and pulling him in deeper, like we were made for each other. Made to do this. Like the past twenty-eight years have been leading up to him pushing inside me and me holding him deep and hard and tight.

His pace is perfection, and his body is godlike. Our hands are everywhere at once, and everything seems to get faster and harder every second. But he keeps his eyes on me…his deep-brown eyes. Those eyes I've known and adored since I was an infant.

I could look at him forever. I could feel him in me, bursting with pleasure and desire and fulfilling every silent need I didn't know I had.

When everything seems to start melting and exploding, he slows down, and I try to catch my breath. And then, Chase Kennedy does something I never imagined was even remotely a part of his sexual repertoire.

He kisses me. Soft and sweet. He strokes my cheek with his hand, admiring me and drinking me in, like he's savoring this moment.

I hold him as he fucks me slowly, kissing me lightly, and I feel an overwhelming swell of emotion rise in my chest—joy, pleasure, excitement…

Love.

No! Jesus Christ, no. I cannot be falling for Chase. He's fucking *Chase.*

I shake off the crashing realization and finally break eye contact, remembering that this has to stay wholly and completely physical, and something tells me soft kisses and longing gazes are going beyond that.

Keep it playful. Keep it sexy.

"You have to teach me something, Six," I tease. "Remember?" I try to keep it light and push off the heavy emotion of the moment by giving his tight ass a nice squeeze.

He draws back with a hint of surprise, still deep inside me, his body infinitely tangled up with mine. "All right." He slides out and lies on his back next to me, still breathing heavily. "Your turn. Hop on."

I roll my eyes and giggle at what is likely the sexiest invitation I've ever had and eagerly straddle his raging boner.

"You're so gorgeous," he says, admiring me with a sense of disbelief, an expression that makes me want to just melt and swim and fall into him.

"How's this doing?" I hold his right shoulder and give it a light, sexy squeeze.

"Feels better now," Chase rasps with an eager nod.

I slide my hand down his diamond-hard abs and then around the length of him, burning with lust and need, our ache for pleasure feeding off each other and sizzling on our sticky skin.

"Like this." He grabs my hips, holding me tight, and pulls me down onto him, his cock once again filling me so deeply my toes curl.

I gasp, and he moans, and everything picks up again in a rapid, desperate rhythm.

Chase guides my hips up and down around him as he thrusts slightly underneath me, sending waves of need crashing over me. Pleasure curls through my spine, and I realize I love this moment more than anything.

I grind and rock my hips on him, feeling him driving into me and watching the explosion of lust spark in his eyes.

Suddenly, I feel consumed by a sexy, wild, reckless need, and I completely let myself go. I ride him hard and fast and follow his hands and eyes and mouth, feeling every sensation getting more and more intense as passion builds and bursts between us.

My heart slams and races, and I moan and smile. Chase smiles, too. We fuck harder and faster, and I realize I've never had so much fun and pleasure and insane primal drive like right now.

He grabs my ass hard and uses my body to thrust into me harder and harder, and I feel another orgasm about to rock me to my core. His enormous length is throbbing inside me, and my whole body squeezes and grips around him.

"Chase—"

"Whit—"

Everything crashes at once. I come hard and feel him releasing into my tight center as we both let the pleasure wash over us.

I collapse onto him, our bodies slick with sweat.

Chase holds me tightly, his fingers clutching my skin, both of us still gripped by the power and intensity of…that.

I press my forehead to his as we both desperately try to catch our breath and slow the rapid beating of our hearts against each other.

Suddenly, we both bubble with laughter, everything about the moment so deeply and passionately intimate, it's as if we both remembered, in the midst of toe-curling orgasms and wild sex, that we're still best friends. We're still decades of inside jokes and hundreds of Bud Lights and a million late-night phone calls.

Fear twinges in my chest, and I quickly roll off of him and curl up under his arm, trying to push away the rise of emotion and thoughts of love that race through my mind.

It was just good sex. Right?

Chase rolls onto his side and wraps me up, tucking my head under his chin and seemingly holding every part of me together with just his hands. "Touchdown."

I laugh and snuggle into him. "Touchdown is right."

He grabs my face quickly and plants a firm, passionate kiss on my lips that sparks with fireworks. "Extra point."

I laugh heartily and take a long, deep breath, feeling every powerful and wonderful thing about having sex with Chase and letting myself drown in him, all of him, for just one night.

In some confusing way, we love each other. In an even more confusing way, we always have.

twenty-five

Chase

I can't tell if I'm awake or asleep. My head is completely lost in a fuzzy daze of relief and comfort and…home. She's in my arms. Tiny and silent and the most preciously peaceful thing I have ever seen or held or…adored. I've never wanted a woman to stay in my bed for too terribly long, but this is different, this is Whitney, and I honestly never want her to leave it.

I pull her into me tightly, inhaling the sweet coconut shampoo she's used since middle school and clinging tightly to this moment.

There's an unfamiliar warmth filling my chest, a weirdly calm sense of peace and happiness that I've sure as hell never gotten from waking up with any other chick before. It wasn't just the sex—the unreal, unbelievable, earth-shaking sex—it was everything. The way she understood my feelings and deep shit about my parents. She made it easy and safe and… okay. She makes everything okay. No, she makes everything fucking wonderful.

And now she's naked in my arms, where she's been all night long, sound asleep, and I'm trying to figure out the most confusing cocktail of feelings that's ever swirled around in my head.

My life is simple. Play football, get laid, stay single, be a total stud. Whitney's my best friend. That's how this shit works. I'm Chase Kennedy, NFL quarterback and notorious heartbreaking womanizer.

But, fuck. Right now, I feel like she could break *my* heart if she wanted to. I need her. And not in the way that I always have, but in this new way now. Maybe Dylan is actually on to something with that *the one* bullshit. Maybe she's been next to me all along. *Holy fuck.*

"Morning, Six." Her voice is soft and sexy and sleepy.

"Hi, Nit Whit," I whisper, suddenly realizing how badly I want to spend the entire day in this bed, with her. My Whit. My best friend. And now, my… something more.

"Last night was—" I've never been good at talking about feelings. Hell, I've never ever really had feelings. But I want to tell her at least what's going through my mind. That she has me questioning my entire life and priorities and wondering if I've ever really even been *happy* until now.

"Fun!" She sits up suddenly, holding the sheet to cover herself. A forced brightness lights up her face, and something about her smile seems nervous. "Thanks for helping me out."

She slips out of the bed and starts to get dressed, and a wave of confused disappointment crashes over me.

Thanks for helping me out? The fuck?

"Uh..." I run a hand through my hair and lean against the headboard, watching her rush to yank her clothes on. "Do you work today?"

"No, I work tomorrow." She smiles dismissively.

I laugh softly. "Then what's the big-ass hurry, Nit Whit?"

She gathers her bag in her arms and looks at me, her eyes filled with something I can't recognize. Confusion? Fear? "What, are we gonna lie here and snuggle? I could be wrong, but I'm pretty sure you're not exactly the snuggly type, Six. Come on."

I push away the lump that rises in my throat. I can't argue with her. I can't deny it. Based on everything Whitney Cooper knows about me, I would want her out of my bed as fast as possible. She would assume I think that was just a fun hookup. A long time coming. But I don't want her to go. And it wasn't a hookup.

"Don't go, Whit." I hate that I sound like I'm fucking begging, but she can't just leave after last night. After...*that.* I attempt to lighten the mood by offering an easy smile.

"Chase..." She bites her lip and looks toward the door. "Our sex lessons are really fun. But we have to keep it at just that. I don't want to..." She swallows and shakes her head. "We just have to keep it strictly physical. Because in less than a week, I'm going on a date with Peter Chapman, who could potentially be a nice, long-term guy for me. And you—" She forces a laugh and twists a strand of chocolate-colored hair. "You can go back to being Chase Kennedy—All-Pro quarterback and renowned king of the...rail and bail, as I believe you've called it?"

I look down at the black sheets and try to figure out how I'll ever want another woman in this bed after last night.

Well, shit. I guess I read something wrong. It was still just fun physical stuff for her. Something sharp twists in my gut as words tumble out of my mouth. "And then what? With, like…us?"

She narrows her eyes, and I swear she's fighting tears. "We're friends, Six. We'll barely even remember all this in a few months."

Okay, we both know that's a fat lie. As if the image of her giant brown eyes exploding with reckless pleasure while she rode my dick like a fucking Harley isn't going to be burned into my mind forever.

I don't want to push her, and I definitely don't want to ever hurt her. And if I really am that fuckboy heartbreaker everyone thinks I am, then that's a very real possibility. "True that, Nit Whit." The words taste wrong.

"Bye, Six," she sings playfully as she bounces out the door, leaving me with a whirlwind of questions and a mix of emotions I've spent twenty-eight years trying to avoid.

I don't love Whitney. I mean, I do. In, like, a best friend way, of course. There's no way I love her, because I'm not *capable* of love. Whitney wants a husband and a lifelong commitment and a poster family behind a white picket fence. Whitney is capable of love. She's capable of everything.

Even if I do maybe love her, it doesn't fucking matter. She'll never see past my sleazy history and the fact that I've banged my way through a line of NFL groupies and never gave a second thought to anyone's…feelings. That's who I am to her. That's who I am to everyone.

I press my palms into my forehead and sink back into the bed.

That's just who I am.

It was all only physical. That's all it's been, ever since I proposed this insane idea that I show her the ropes in bed. I'm still trying to decide if that's the best or worst idea I've ever had.

I know one thing for sure. I'm not done. Nothing is going to make sense until I make love to her again. I mean, *have sex* with her. Plow her. Whatever.

So what if it's strictly physical? I need it. I need her. In so many weird, confusing, and incredible ways. I need her.

twenty-six

Whitney

I resent you, tear. Stupid hot useless drop of saltwater falling down my cheek for absolutely *no* definable reason. Go away.

I fumble with the keys in the ignition and take a long, deep breath. I can't be falling for Chase. But, shit, I can't *help* falling for Chase. Every inch of him is pure, unadulterated magic.

Why does it feel like so much more than just sex? It twists my gut to think of how on point Melody's prediction was. I totally dismissed it, assuming there was absolutely no way I could ever develop *feelings* for Chase Kennedy.

I whip out of the parking garage in his apartment building and curse my painfully naïve past self.

Among the dizzying, messy blur that surrounds these past few weeks with Chase, I try to force myself to see clearly and remember exactly why I agreed to this absurdity in the first place. Do I really want to be prepared for the dating world and impress Peter if and when we get intimate?

Or was I just subconsciously trying to finally get into bed with the man I've been in love with for twenty years?

"Shit," I whisper as I accelerate onto the highway. The sky is a rare gray overcast, and the streets of South Florida seem to lack their usual sparkling, sunny warmth.

The drive home is slow, and I don't even bother turning on the radio. There's no way to escape this confusing mess of feelings and get back on track to exactly who I am and what I want. And *who* I want.

Well, there's one way. I need to get Chase off my mind.

As I pull into Melody's townhouse complex, I park in a spot in front of our unit and take my phone out of my bag. There's a text from Melody that she sent last night, but I didn't see it until now. Sorry, Mel. I was a little busy.

Remember, cuz. STAY STRONG!

She followed it with a series of colorful emojis, including a man lifting weights and an arm with a flexed bicep.

I blow out an exasperated sigh and shake my head, remembering why I took my phone out in the first place.

I tap on the phone button, scanning through my recent calls, trying not to notice how many of them are from Chase, and find Peter's UK number.

My thumb hovers over the screen while I quickly attempt to do some math and figure out what time it is in London.

Screw it.

I hit call. The ringing sound gets my heart skipping

and a nervous tightness rising in my chest. I lean forward in the driver's seat and press the phone to my ear, not sure what I want more: his voice or no answer.

"This is Peter Chapman." His deep voice makes me jump slightly, and his professional and hurried tone makes me massively regret calling.

"Hey, Peter, you're probably totally busy. I just thought I'd try you. It's Whitney," I add quickly with a pathetically awkward laugh.

"Whitney," he draws my name out, and I can practically hear a slow smile coming across his handsome face.

I feel a slight wash of relief. "How's London?" My tone comes out high-pitched and cheery, ringing fake in my own ears.

"Oh, you know. Multimillion-dollar contracts and angry investors. Par for the course, as usual. The city is quite special, although I've grown so accustomed to it that I really just want to get back to the States in a few days."

I force a smile onto my face even though I know he can't see me. "Well, South Florida misses you. And I can't wait for our date! I keep thinking about it."

He chuckles, and I hear people chatting in the background. He must be outside or something. "Is that so, Whitney Cooper?"

"Oh yeah." I lean against the steering wheel and run my hand through my hair. "It's what's getting me through some of these brutal twelve-hour shifts at the ER." I silently try to convince myself that's not a lie. That Peter is the guy of my dreams. Because he is. He checks every single box. Whereas freaking Six…he laughs and rips up the list of criteria. And then screws me so good I can't think straight.

"I'm glad to hear that. I'm really looking forward to it, as well. It will be an absolute privilege to get to know you better and see where things could go."

"Yes, me, too." I make a conscious effort to sound mature and sophisticated, like some high-class socialite woman who would catch the eye of someone like Peter Hedge Fund Manager Chapman.

"Well, Miss Cooper, it was an absolute pleasure to hear from you. But I do have to run. Investors meeting awaits," he says.

"Of course! Have fun investing." I add a self-deprecating laugh, still really unsure of what exactly his job consists of. I suppose that will be clarified on our date.

"Bye, Whitney. Can't wait to see you again." He hangs up the phone, and I drop my forehead onto the top of the steering wheel, letting out a defeated groan.

I'm not really sure what I was trying to accomplish by calling Peter, but I don't feel a whole lot better.

It must be because he's so far away. It must be because we've actually hung out and talked in person only one time at that silly party, and I'm forgetting how strong our connection was that night.

Right?

It'll all come back when we go out on our nice, fancy, classy-ass dinner date, and I'll remember why I got into this whole mess in the first place, and any shred of a crush or feelings or...*love* for Chase will completely disappear.

Because Peter is the right guy for me. He's steady and mature and ready for commitment. Chase is...I mean, Christ, he's *Chase*! He's reckless and wild and cocky and my asshole of a best friend. Letting myself fall for Chase would be the biggest risk of heartbreak imaginable.

I don't want heartbreak. I want forever. And I don't think any amount of mind-blowing sex or inside jokes or deep conversations could convince Chase Kennedy that *forever* is even an option.

twenty-seven

Chase

"So it's a fake handoff to Danes and then a delayed long pass to Sterling through the slot?" Matt McKenzie squints and holds a hand up to shield his eyes from the blazing sun.

I nod and wipe a drop of sweat from my forehead. "Yeah. And don't get your ass sacked. Which goes without saying, but, you know. You think you can handle pressure, and then you're out there."

Practice today is longer and hotter than usual, and running through offenses with my bright-eyed potential replacement isn't my favorite activity. Still, the rookie kid is kinda growing on me. A little bit. He respects me and sees me as more than just the obnoxiously arrogant playboy quarterback. He looks up to me, and I like that.

"Okay, cool. I think I got it." Matt nods enthusiastically. "Thanks, Kennedy."

I smack his helmet. "Yeah, yeah."

"Bring it in!" Coach Watson blows his whistle and bellows the order from down the field.

Thank fuck. It's hotter than the devil's sack out here, and my mood isn't exactly peachy. I can't stop thinking about that weird, gritty emptiness I felt when Whitney left yesterday morning. The way she so casually mentioned me going back to my old ways. I mean, my *normal* ways. I should be stoked.

I'm not.

"I owe you another thanks." Matt jogs to catch up with me as we head into the locker room.

I pull off my helmet and shake out my hair. "And what would that be for, Junior?"

"You know." He nods and lowers his voice, like we have some kind of boys club secret. "The other night."

"Oh right. The actress. Abigail whatever."

"Arabella." Matt's eyes widen when he says her name.

"What, did she take your virginity or something?" I roll my eyes as we swing the door open and walk to our lockers.

"No, asshole," he says through a chuckle. "I was a college QB, remember?"

I chug a bottle of Gatorade and give Matt a rough pat on the shoulder. "I'm just fucking with you. Glad you had a good time."

"Yeah. A damn good time." We stand in front of our lockers, which, of fucking course, are right next to each other since we play the same position. I really can't escape the rookie puppy dog, can I?

"Good thing you have a girlfriend." Matt swings open his locker and nods at me. "Or you definitely would not have gifted me such a golden slam opportunity."

“I have a gir—” The word literally sticks in my throat. “A *what*?”

“Your girlfriend…” Matt angles his head toward me and furrows his brow. “The hot nurse you’re always laughing with? I saw her waiting outside the tunnel for you after the last home game. She’s not your girl?”

My chest feels tight, and an unpleasant whirlwind of confusion rips through my brain. “Whitney’s my best friend, dipshit. I don’t have a fucking *girlfriend*.”

“Shit, man.” Matt holds up his hands defensively. “My bad. You two just seem to have that connect-y thing. That couple thing. The way you look at her. I thought that’s why you were being my wingman and giving me some single-life tips. Kinda passing on all the knowledge from your glory days.”

I narrow my eyes, trying to identify the feeling stabbing into my gut. A part of me wants to deck Junior right in his baby face. But a weird sense of hope twists through my head.

I turn back to my locker and yank off my practice jersey, leaning my palm against the cold metal and clenching my jaw. I look at Matt, already in shock from the words that are about to come out of my mouth. “You think I could have a girlfriend?”

Who the fuck am I?

Matt frowns and laughs in confusion. “Uh, yeah? I for sure thought you did.”

“Huh. Well, we’re just friends, Whit and me,” I say, my words slow and unconvincing.

Best friends. Who are banging. Sleeping together. Making love.

Jesus Christ, Kennedy.

"Thought you said it was complicated," Dylan interjects, walking up to us with a practice jersey slung over his bare shoulder.

"Don't you have a soccer ball to go kick around, Rivera?"

He rolls his eyes and dismisses my comment, turning to Matt. "Listen, McKenzie. You think you know Chase, but you don't. You know what you've heard and the little bit you've seen of him since you got drafted. But our No. 6 here is truly the most soulless motherfucker to ever walk the earth." They both laugh. "Kennedy will have a *committed girlfriend* the day we play the Super Bowl on the moon. And even then, he'd rather find some hot alien to smash and never talk to again."

Matt shakes his head in awe and sits on the bench. "Damn, dude. Sounds like you're even more of a legend than I originally thought."

I drop onto the bench next to him and lean down to untie the laces on my cleats. I keep my gaze fixed on the floor, unsure why Dylan's description of me is pissing me off so much. He's spot-on. That's exactly who I've always been.

But yesterday, when Whit left, I didn't feel like that guy. I didn't feel like me. I wanted to be something else…something more.

Dylan leans against the bench across from us and checks his phone, giving me a quizzical look. Other than Whitney, Dylan can read me faster and more accurately than anyone else. "You good, bro?"

"It is complicated," I blurt out without a second thought. "With Whitney. It's really confusing, and I feel…I feel some shit. It's fucked up."

"'I feel some shit. It's fucked up,'" Dylan repeats through a hearty laugh. "Is this the Chase Kennedy way of admitting you *like* her?"

Dylan moves over and sits closer so he, Matt, and I are in a small circle, and no one can hear our conversation. Leo and Elliot can't hear this. They'll get way too excited and take me ring shopping or some shit.

"All right, assholes. Here's the deal. She and I have been fooling around."

"This doesn't shock me," Dylan says flatly.

"Right. Well, I've been kind of…helping her. Teaching her, I guess. How to do everything and be more adventurous in the sack."

Matt's jaw drops. "That's hot as fuck."

"Cram it, Junior. Point is, I feel like it's getting to be more than that. And I've never done more than that, or felt more than that, or even come close to being more than that with anyone. Ever."

"Do you want to, like, *be* with her?" Dylan leans forward. "Are you even capable of that?"

I swallow, knowing his jab was just a joke, but feeling the truth hit my gut hard. "Honestly? I don't fucking know."

"How much have you guys been banging?" Matt asks.

"Only once." I run a hand through my hair, realizing how bizarre this is going to sound to my teammates. "We've been sort of…working up to it. Baby steps, I guess."

Dylan chokes on a surprised laugh. "The man who regularly has three-ways with cheerleaders and rotates a roster of supermodels is taking *baby steps*?"

I kick him in the shin. "Fuck off. She's different. She's still my best friend."

I hope. It sure didn't feel like it when she left yesterday.

Matt shrugs. "There's only one obvious way to figure out what the hell is going on."

"All right, wise one." I turn to him. "Enlighten me."

He and Dylan share a look, as if this is something stupidly apparent that I'm just missing. "You have to pipe her again. Maybe it was just a mixed-up thing because you guys have always been so close, and now getting physical is making it confusing," Matt says, shrouded in a weird level of maturity.

"Or…" Dylan points a finger at me. "She's the one. And you just didn't realize it until now."

"Christ, not that bullshit again," I groan.

"The one?" Matt chuckles.

"Everybody has a one," Dylan says with his charming, sweet-boy smile.

"You idiots might have a point." I run my thumb across my jawline and stand up. "I guess sex could clarify some shit."

Besides, I can't say I'm terribly opposed to repeating the most explosive and passionate and sinfully hot lay I've ever had. Only problem is, I don't know if Whit will jump back into my sex sheets with zero hesitation.

"Holy shit." Matt stands up and turns back to his locker. "I just gave Chase Kennedy advice."

I slam my locker door shut and turn to him. "Don't jerk yourself off too hard yet, Junior. If my situation gets even more screwed up because of you, I'm gonna beat your ass."

I tighten and stretch my right shoulder, which is basically better. There's only a tiny little twinge of pain at certain angles now, but I better ask Whitney to come over tonight and make sure it's okay.

Just in case.

twenty-eight

Whitney

"So, tonight's the big night. Hedge Fund Guy." Melody digs her toes into the sand as the ocean crashes in front of us and the sun beats down onto my skin.

I take a deep breath of the salty beach air and lean my hands into the soft warmth of the ground. "His name is Peter, not Hedge Fund Guy. And yes, he got back from London this morning, and we're going to dinner. It's not an enormous deal."

She lifts her bedazzled sunglasses onto her head and gives me some serious side-eye. "Cuz, you've literally been planning this for a month. A freaking month. You're so jazzed about this guy you asked Chase Kennedy for *sex* lessons and..." She turns back to the ocean, suddenly realizing that notion isn't as humorous and lighthearted as it was originally. "Well, anyway. I'm excited for you."

I swallow the thoughts and images of Chase and watch as a wave splashes onto the sand. "Right now, I'm just happy to be lying on the beach with my favorite cousin." I give her a cheesy grin to lighten the mood.

Melody rests her head on my shoulder and lightly kicks a pile of sand, not getting my *please lighten the mood* cue. "How are you feeling about all of that craziness? You told me you guys did the ol' *deed*, but you spared gory details, and frankly, I'm offended. And hella curious."

I puff out a breath, shutting my eyes and letting the heat of the sun wrap itself around me. "I don't even know, Mel. It was…" I open my eyes and watch the water, feeling a rush of emotion and turning to my eccentric yet highly compassionate cousin. "It was incredible. Mind-blowing. Unbelievable."

"More than just physical," she says quietly.

I purse my lips and gaze back out at the sea. "I tried to shut my feelings off. To squash that little seed of a crush before it grew into something else. But I couldn't. There was this…passion. This intensity. It felt so special and real. It was palpable. But then I wonder…" I bite my lip and fight the emotion in my throat. "Is that just how he does it? Because he's… Chase?"

"Well, shit monkeys, cuz. You fell for him after all."

"I don't know if I necessarily *fell*. I just—"

Suddenly, my phone vibrates and lights up next to me on the beach towel.

"Speak of the damn devil," I say slowly as my eyes scan a message from Chase. The first communication I've had with him since I left yesterday morning.

Hey, Nit Whit. Having some shoulder issues. Kinda worried. Can you make it over tonight? Need my nurse/good luck charm/favorite homie. :)

Hope sparks in my chest at the thought of our friendship staying preserved through all of this messy weirdness. That hope is instantly met by a wash of fear and confusion.

What if friendship is never enough again? What if I can never truly shake these feelings?

"Gimme!" Melody snatches the phone, and her eyes widen as she gasps dramatically and reads the text.

"I should probably go." The words slip out before I can think clearly. "I mean, what if he's really hurt? No one else knows about this injury—"

"Injury, my ass!" Melody hands the phone back to me with a look of wild excitement sparking in her expression. "What if this is *fate*? He realized you're the one!"

I snort and mindlessly play with a pile of sand under my feet. "You're insane, Melody."

"You have to go." She grabs my shoulders and shakes me vigorously. "You have to! What if Chase is your guy? What if Chase is your forever?"

"Chase. Chase, who I've singlehandedly watched bang his way through South Florida? Chase, who had two homecoming dates? Chase, who is physically incapable of feeling anything beyond 'who can I shove it in today'?"

"You said you thought he felt it, too. When you guys slept together. What if he really did? He adores you more than anything in the universe. Plus, he's a Taurus."

I frown and stare at her.

Her jaw drops, and she raises her brows at me. "They fall in love the hardest. Duh."

I gather my beach bag and tie my hair up in a bun. "I'm gonna go. To help him with his *shoulder*." I give

Melody a stern look. "And for no reason other than that."

I stand and pick up my towel, shaking the sand off and fighting the swarm of butterflies that released in my stomach at the spontaneous plan to see Chase tonight.

"Whatever you need to tell yourself," Melody teases in a singsong voice. "Maybe you'll just have to do a little more…" She gives an exaggerated wink and holds up air quotes. "'*Practicing.*'"

I shove her playfully as she stands up to walk back to the townhouse with me.

"No matter what we're feeling or thinking or…*doing*," I explain to Melody as we walk down the sidewalk, "Chase is still my best friend. And when we started this whole big mess, we agreed our friendship would not waver. I have to hold up my end of that. Before we got physical, I'd be there for him in a second, no questions asked. So that's what I'm doing tonight."

Being there for my best friend. For his *shoulder.* Not his deep-brown eyes, or his sinful mouth, or any other unbelievably flawless part of his body. Or his heart.

"Mm-hmm. Okay." She flips her pink hair and arches a brow. "You're sleeping with him again tonight."

"Mel, I'm going out with Peter tonight. All my attention is completely focused on that. My *lessons* with Chase are over and done with."

My own words stab my chest with sharp jabs of disappointment, but I know it's what's best. My heart has never been the most discerning decision-maker, and every synapse of my brain is way too familiar with the habits of Chase Kennedy to ever even think about going for him.

Still, I'd be lying if I said I didn't feel the tiniest little achy excitement swirl down my spine at the thought of us doing it one last time tonight.

For practice.

twenty-nine

Chase

I clench my jaw tight and look out over the skyline. The sun is still shining bright. It's only early afternoon. Leaning against the glass, I shake out my hair, still damp from the shower I took after texting Whitney.

I stretch my shoulder to see if there's any real pain, or if I'm just so completely fucked up in the head that I had to pretend it hurts to get her to come over. Just to see her.

Babyface is right. I need to bang her another time to figure out what's going on with me. Or with us, or whatever. All I really know for sure is that it's amazing, and I don't want it to end. I also know that I feel like some weird, new version of myself. And I don't want to go back to how I was before.

Which is freaky, but kinda nice. Maybe I'm not as much of a jackass as everyone thinks I am. Maybe I can have feelings and make something that lasts. Maybe it's Whitney. Maybe it's been her my entire life, and it just took getting physical for me to realize it.

I pace nervously around the living room.

I'm fucking *pacing*. Like a fourteen-year-old girl waiting for the cute senior boy to come pick her up for prom. Jesus Christ.

I slump down on the couch and pinch the bridge of my nose. I wish I could stop seeing that stupid Volvo backing out of the driveway when I was thirteen and hearing echoes of my dad telling me, *All that love bullshit isn't real.*

I've had fun. I've been around the block more than a few times. But now, all I want is my freckle-cheeked best friend, who knows every layer of me like the back of her hand and makes my mind and body and heart spark with fireworks.

I hear the door handle click and stand up to walk toward her.

"Hi, Six."

Whitney has a flowery sundress on with blue bikini straps pulled around her neck underneath it. She's pink and glowing, like she's been kissed all over by the sun. Her skin looks like silk, and every perfect curve is delicately wrapped in a sundress that *needs* to come off.

"Hi, Nit Whit."

She walks past me and into the kitchen, getting a glass from the cabinet and filling it with water. "I was at the beach with Melody when I saw your text. I didn't shower or change in case this was some kind of…" She smiles and arches a brow at me, exploring my shirtless body with her gaze. "Emergency."

I cock my head and smile, leaning against the kitchen counter next to her. "You smell like sunscreen."

She rolls her eyes and sips the water. "I burn easily, asshole. Also, you don't exactly look like you're in gut-wrenching pain."

I bite my lower lip and inch closer to her, feeling the warm pull of attraction yanking at every part of my body and sending blood south very quickly. "It feels a little better now."

"Chase!" She smacks my bicep and stifles a laugh. "I'm here as a medical professional."

I hold the string of her bikini strap with two fingers and give it a light snap against her delicate collarbone. "You're not dressed like a medical professional."

Her lips part seductively, contrasting with the playful annoyance in her eyes. "You said you *needed* me." She's practically whispering, and somehow our mouths are about three centimeters apart.

Three centimeters too many.

I move my hands up the sides of her flawlessly toned body, the smooth material of her dress sliding easily over her skin. "I do need you, Whit."

"Damn it," she gasps, leaning into my not-very-subtle hard-on. "Why can't I resist you?"

Whitney throws her arms around me and plants her lips on mine, kissing me rapidly and desperately and hard.

I'm flooded by relief and a rushing feeling that I can compare only to throwing a game-winning Hail Mary bullet in the fourth quarter.

I pick her up, and she wraps her legs around my hips, our lips locked, our tongues dancing in and out of each other's mouths. We laugh through our kiss as I almost knock over a really expensive lamp carrying her to the bedroom.

I don't give a shit about anything but her. Kissing her, touching her, making love to her. It's all I want to do.

I ease her onto the bed, and her giggle is like music. As I climb on top of her, heat rages between us, and frantic, wild desire grips our bodies.

Whitney tugs at the waistband of my sweats, kissing my neck and squirming underneath me. Her eyes are wide and passionate, and I cup her cheek, savoring every ounce of perfection that's lying under me.

I slip off the sundress, exposing the soft, tanned, gorgeous woman I've loved for twenty-eight years. I just never knew how much.

I shift her hips, and she rocks against me, waves of hypnotizing attraction coursing through us and between us.

My dick is harder than granite, and my hands can't physically get enough of her.

She arches her back and turns her head into the pillow, smiling and gasping and radiating sexy, feminine sunshine.

"Just one more time," she whispers breathlessly. Her brows are worried, and her face is flushed. "Just one more… Then friends again. Right?"

I draw back, frowning at her and feeling a sudden icy chill fall over the burning heat crackling in this bed. Words pour out of my mouth, her familiar sparkly eyes making it impossible to hesitate or even think about what I say. "I don't want one more time. I want a thousand more. A million." I hold her face with both hands, fixing my gaze on hers and channeling every last drop of romance…of *love*…I didn't even know I was capable of. "Whitney, I've never felt like this. You're everything to me. I—"

"Stop." She scoots out from under me and draws the blanket over her half-naked body. "Stop, Chase." Her voice breaks, and I feel something rip in my chest. "This started as just fun, with you teaching me. I never wanted it to get so—"

"No, it didn't." I shake my head. "It didn't start as me teaching you. It started twenty-eight years ago when we were just little blobs. It continued through every failed exam, every shitty football game, every stupid-drunk night, every time I wanted to punch a wall after my mom left. It was always you."

Tears drop down Whitney's face, and fuck, I might cry, too.

"Six," she whispers, looking down and clutching the blanket tight in her hands. "I just…I know you too well. You think you feel something real, but you don't. You're not ready for what I want. You're mixing up friendship and sex… We both are." She looks away and fights more tears. "I want marriage. Commitment. A family. I want forever."

"I just want you," I plead. "I know that I do."

She runs her fingers through my hair and draws in a slow, shaky breath. "You're always going to be my best friend, Chase Kennedy. But I'm meeting Peter at Ricardo's in a few hours, and we have to just get back to friendship. Nothing more. You have to go be a sleazy NFL playboy, and I have to find a husband. We can't fight who we are."

"I don't even know who I am anymore," I mutter.

Whitney stands up and pulls her dress back on, and my throat is too tight to even attempt to say anything.

I shut my eyes and see my mother's Volvo whip out of the driveway again.

Maybe Whitney's right. Maybe I'll never be capable of anything beyond one-night stands and casual hookups. But for the first time in my entire life, I just want to try. I just want a chance.

But I can't take a chance of hurting Whitney.

"Please, Six?" She ties her hair up on top of her head. "You're my best friend. Can we just wipe all of this away and go back to Bud Light and *South Park*?"

I stand and do the one thing that's always felt like the right thing to do. The only thing to do. I give her a big, tight, happy hug, lifting her off the ground and laughing softly in spite of the rising lump in my throat and stinging behind my eyes.

She laughs, too, and for a nanosecond it seems like maybe everything could go back to normal. And the next nanosecond, it hits me hard how much I don't want that to happen.

I set her down lightly and pull away, smiling at the beautiful, strong, hilarious woman who looks and feels more like home than any penthouse apartment ever could. "Try not to fall asleep at the table when Cubicle Guy starts talking about spreadsheets."

She smacks me playfully, and her eyes flicker with conflict and uncertainty. "I can't make it to the Riders game on Sunday. I got scheduled at the hospital and couldn't get it changed. I'm sorry."

I shrug, fighting the heavy disappointment in my gut. "I guess our agreement is officially over anyway, right?"

She walks out of the bedroom and toward the front

door, and I walk with her, feeling like the ground is covered in water or quicksand or some shit.

She turns to me in front of the door, forcing a smile that I've known Whitney way too long to believe is even remotely real. "Your shoulder is fine. Rookie Boy is no threat. You're still a superstar. And my best friend!" she adds quickly.

Getting stuck in Whitney's friend zone has never bothered or even fazed me, but now I can't imagine how it'll ever be okay.

I lean forward and kiss her softly on the forehead, squeezing my eyes shut and swallowing the harsh pang of jealousy at the thought of some boring-ass finance douchebag getting my girl. "Drive safe, Nit Whit."

She looks at me with a mixture of sadness and love. "Bye, Six."

She walks out.

The door shuts, and I press my palms against it, leaning my forehead against the wood and clenching my jaw tightly.

I want to fight her on this, more than anything, but what if she's right? After all, she does know me better than I know myself. Much better.

Dylan was right.

She's the one.

And I know she's falling for me, too, but shit, I don't ever want to hurt her. I could never hurt her. But she'll never be able to see me as more than her cocky jackass of a best friend. A fuckboy with a room of football trophies and a mile-long list of meaningless hookups. And face it, isn't that exactly who I really am?

I'll never be a safe option, no matter how much we both want to change that.

I walk over to the sofa and lie down, rubbing my forehead and feeling more confused than ever. I pull my phone out of my pocket and stare at it, knowing I'm gonna have to bite the bullet and ask for an assist on this.

Leo Sterling. He was kinda similar to me, back in the day. Not of my caliber, of course, but still a pretty well-known womanizer. Now he's got a baby on the way, and he and his wife could teach classes on how to be a perfect couple.

I run my hand through my hair and click the call button next to his contact info.

He picks up after a couple of rings. "If you need me to bail you out of jail, you're gonna have to call Danes. He's still the nice one."

"Shut up, dickhead. I need some advice, I guess."

Sterling laughs. "This is a first. I thought you knew everything."

"Yeah, well. Not about this." I sit up and lean forward, already in shock from the words I haven't even said out loud yet. "How did you know Frankie was…the…you know…"

"The one?" he finishes.

"Yeah. That. How did you know she was the one?" I feel a sense of relief once the phrase is out of my mouth. Like I am actually capable of thinking and saying and *feeling* that.

"Now *this* is a first," he says slowly, clearly loving the satisfaction of knowing he's not the only high-and-mighty playboy who fell on his face for a certain woman. "Let me guess…"

"Please don't," I interject.

He ignores me. "Your hot-piece-of-ass best friend who you're completely in love with but way too much of a pussy to admit it?"

"Hey!" I hear Frankie shout from a distance on the other end of the phone call. "Watch your mouth around the baby."

"The baby's not born yet, kid," Leo says to his wife with a loving laugh. "So…" He continues. "Am I right, Kennedy?"

"Could you just answer the question and stop being an ass?" I guess we both know that means he's right. Am I that obvious?

"Okay." Leo takes a deep breath. "I knew Frankie was the one when I realized that I would never be complete without her. The moment I felt like every second that wasn't shared with her was total crap. I guess…when I realized that the first twenty-eight years of my life I was just waiting to love her, and once I did, nothing else would ever be enough. Nothing would compare."

"Awww!" I hear Frankie coo from the other room.

I've been waiting to love Whitney. All these years, she's been right in front of me, and I've just been waiting to realize it.

I feel my heart rate pick up, and I jump up off the couch, fueled by a rush of adrenaline and clarity. "Thanks, Sterling. That's exactly what I needed."

"Go get her, bro. I'm proud of you, Kennedy."

I roll my eyes and laugh. "Yeah, save the dad talk for when your offspring arrives."

"Peace out, asshole." He chuckles and hangs up,

leaving me with an electric buzz and a potentially terrible and crazy idea. I don't care if it's crazy.

I rush to my closet and pull on a Riders T-shirt and shove my feet into some Nikes. I'm going to the damn restaurant. I have to get my girl.

thirty

Chase

In the least stalkerish way possible, I pull into the restaurant parking lot, wondering what the hell is even going through my psychotic mind. I park far from the front windows so Whitney won't instantly see my bright green Lambo.

I don't even know what I'm going to say. I don't even know what I'm doing here. All I know is that I'm in love with Whitney, and I think I have been for a long-ass time. I know I'm not exactly boyfriend material, and definitely not husband material, but she has to feel it, too, right? She'll take a chance with me.

I sure as hell hope she will, because I don't think our friendship can really ever go back to how it was after everything that's happened. Definitely not after I crash her fancy, important date.

I step out of my car, suddenly wishing the vehicle weren't so painfully eye-catching. A rush of nerves rises in my chest, and I do my best to swallow it and pull my shit together.

I've never in my life had a woman turn me down. And I've also never in my life been so unbelievably scared of rejection. Everything Leo said feels true for Whitney and me. I need her. I can't go on living without her being mine. She has to be mine.

I pause outside the restaurant, hidden behind a wall but getting a clear shot through the window.

Of course it's one of those snooty, pretentious places where people send their wine back and the chef tells you what to eat. Whit hates places like this. Right?

I'm physically incapable of pulling my gaze away from her and douchepants at their little table in the corner.

God, she's beautiful. Her head tilts as she laughs, and I can hear the musical sound of it. An electric current ripples through me as I look at her.

"Shit," I whisper as the realization of what I'm looking at hits me harder than a linebacker sacking my ass in a play.

She's laughing. Talking with him. She looks so damn *happy*, at least from where I'm standing.

But she's mine. She has to be with me.

I narrow my eyes and clench my jaw, feeling a wave of disappointment roll through my body.

That's him, all right. That's Whitney's textbook husband material. Clean-cut, obviously wealthy, stable, ready for a wife and some babies and a damn picket fence.

He reaches for her hand, and my gut twists.

I should really look away. I should really just leave.

He picks up her hand and slowly draws it toward his mouth, giving it a soft kiss.

I frown and stop breathing as I watch her reaction. She giggles, looking at him like he hung the damn stars. Like he's everything she wants and everything she deserves.

I swallow the lump in my throat and walk back to my stupid car. A single raindrop smacks me on the nose, and I wipe it off angrily.

As I get into the car—the spacecraft, as Whitney calls it—I slump down in the seat and realize what I should have realized before I even left my apartment tonight.

Taking Whitney would be insanely selfish. This guy, this suit-wearing, world-traveling, spreadsheet-making guy… This is who she wants. The perfect, mature, ready-to-go husband who's never broken a heart in his life.

"I'm sorry, Whitney," I whisper, like a crazy person, knowing what I have to do and hating that it's come to this.

I have to let Whitney go. I have to let her be free of me—sex, friendship, love—all of it. She has to go and find her perfectly red-flagless forever dude, and I'd truly be a self-centered piece of shit if I stole that opportunity from her.

She's laughing, she's happy. She likes this guy, and I need to let her. And I know for a damn fact that trying to continue our friendship after all the intense shit we've shared these past few weeks will destroy both of us.

I'm such a chickenshit for this, I know, but I can't face her. Her brown eyes make me do crazy things, and I need to do the *right* thing.

I dig through the glovebox and find my spiral

notebook I use to jot down new plays after practice. I tear out a piece of paper and grab a pen, scribbling a note on it that I hope explains my reasoning. I write that I'm letting her go, that I love her, for real, but this has to be the end. She deserves Mr. Right, and I can't get in the way of that.

I step out of my car and feel another single raindrop hit my forehead as I tuck the note under the windshield wiper of her white Honda Civic.

As I'm walking back, another drop rolls down my cheek. I flick it away with my thumb, knowing damn well that one wasn't rain.

thirty-one

Whitney

Is he about to kiss my hand? God, I hate shit like that.

I adamantly remind myself to give it a chance. Give it a fair, honest, open-minded chance.

I giggle and lean my head back, hoping some fake happiness and excitement will turn into the real thing. They don't.

As soon as Perfect Peter's lips touch my hand, I just want to retract it instantly. I want Chase's lips on my hand. And everywhere else. I knew I was going after Peter all along, so why does it feel so horribly wrong right now?

I stab a piece of lettuce with my fork and force a sweet smile. Of course it's the fancy kind of lettuce that comes in dark green and purple and has curly ends.

What the hell is wrong with me? I'm on an expensive dinner date with one of South Florida's most eligible bachelors, who is completely and totally *enamored* of me, and I'm thinking about Chase freaking Kennedy.

His body, his voice, his perfect, magical, wildly confusing heart. His bizarre plea for us to be together last night. He opened a door in my mind when he said those things. He planted a seed that I can*not* let grow.

Peter, dumbass. Focus on Peter.

"So, anyway, I guess that's the inherent dichotomy of the culture in Brussels." Peter swirls his wine and angles his head toward me.

Did he just *sniff* his wine before drinking it?

I force a bright laugh. "That's incredible, Peter. I sure do envy how well-traveled you are. Unfortunately, ER nurse isn't exactly a profession that sends you around the globe on business."

He wrinkles his nose in mock disgust. "I seriously don't know how you do that. Blood and illness… yuck. I can't think of anything worse. No offense, I mean, it's quite noble. Why *do* you do it, Whitney Cooper?"

I suddenly have a burning desire for him to stop calling me by my first and last name.

"The paycheck," I say sarcastically, delicately placing some bougie lettuce into my mouth.

He chuckles and sips the wine. "Seriously, though?"

I lean back in the dark red leather seat, scanning the unnecessarily glitzy décor of the restaurant, ignoring the voice in my head that screams about how much I'd rather be drinking Bud Lights and eating Domino's with Chase. "It sounds cliché, but I really do like helping people." I look down at my annoyingly small portion of salad, then back up at Peter. "Caring for sick and injured patients is obviously a rush and more rewarding than anything, but it's more than that. I feel like my job is one of the only ones where you can actually physically save a life with your own two hands. Or at least change it."

"You are a fascinating woman," he says slowly, as if he's evaluating me somehow.

Discomfort makes me ramble, so I keep going. "One time, I had a pregnant woman come in, frantic. She had started…" I stop myself from using medical terms at a high-class restaurant with a hedge fund manager. "The, uh, labor process in the cab, and I delivered the baby right in the emergency room. It was a girl, and the mother named her Whitney. After me. She said I was her angel."

My mind dives into a flashback of the moment before Chase kissed me the first time. First down. When he said he thinks our salaries should be switched. I smile to myself and feel a palpable ache for him.

Peter raises his brows and draws back.

Filling silence again, I add, "I guess that's just an example of why I do it. Why I love it."

"You save lives, you deliver babies. You're like Wonder Woman. Which, of course, begs the question…" He leans forward and narrows his eyes. "Why on earth are you still single, Whitney Cooper?"

I cringe slightly.

Hmm. I don't know, Peter. Maybe because I only recently realized that I've been subconsciously in love with my total jackass of a best friend for the past twenty-eight years, and deep down I know that no one and nothing will ever come close to how he makes me feel.

I lift a shoulder and laugh dryly. "Poor taste, I guess."

He lifts his glass and holds it up between us. "To improving our taste."

I hesitantly pick up my wine glass and tap it to his, my head awash with an image of Chase shotgunning a beer in my dorm room freshman year of college and then burping so loud I screamed. I stifle a laugh at the memory. "Cheers to that, Peter."

"You know…" He swirls his wine *again* and half smiles at me. "If things do, let's say for argument's sake, end up working out between us…"

I notice the amount of gel in his hair and get the sudden urge to dump a glass of water on it.

"You wouldn't have to work that brutal job anymore." He nods slowly. "You could just be my traveling companion. See the sights, drink in the entirety of the earth and all it has to offer. That's what you deserve, Whitney Cooper."

I swallow hard and feel a ripple of rage curl through my stomach. "What?" I laugh through my irritation. "Peter, I *love* my job. I would never quit."

"Of course." He draws back defensively. "I'm just saying, you could take a bunch of time off. I mean, you make pennies anyway."

When you think about it, Whit, our salaries should really be switched.

I ache for him again. Shit.

I frown in disgust and try to slow my increasing heart rate and pick my jaw up. "You don't get me at all, do you?"

"Whitney, I just meant—"

"No." I hold up a hand, shaking my head slowly and feeling clarity crash into me like a wave in the ocean. "You don't get me. You'll never get me. I'm sorry, Peter. I'm not..." I gesture around the restaurant and at the wickedly overpriced glasses of Chardonnay. "This isn't me. I love my job. I don't care about the European cultural dichotomy. I'm..."

Supposed to be with Chase.

"Please." He reaches out to touch my hand. "I'm sorry, I—"

"I have to go. I have...work tomorrow." I stand up and nervously fix my hair, unsure of what electric emotion has come over me. "Thanks for dinner."

I grab my purse and hurry out of the restaurant, walking recklessly into a torrential downpour that's pounding the streets and soaking every inch of grass. I didn't even notice it starting to drizzle, but the parking lot is quickly becoming a lake.

I can barely catch my breath.

No rash decisions, Whitney.

I'm practically jogging to my car, water sloshing under my feet and making me wish I'd worn sneakers and not these stupid heels. I wipe the mascara running down my face in black rivers, and my hair is stuck all over me.

I don't care. Chase is it. Chase is the one.

I can barely see in front of me through the rain as I finally find my car and notice a white piece of paper stuck on the windshield.

"Goddammit," I groan. "A freaking parking ticket? I paid the meter!" I wipe a strand of wet hair off of my face.

Wondering how this night could possibly get worse, I snag the paper and duck into my car, dripping water everywhere.

It's not a parking ticket. It's a lined piece of notebook paper, completely saturated from the rain. I unfold it slowly, feeling my heart pounding nervously in my chest.

My hands quiver slightly as I open it, my gut screaming at me that this has something to do with Chase. My Chase.

It's a black blur, water stains soaking through the paper, making it impossible to read. The only words I can make out are right at the bottom, where the edge of the paper had been tucked under the wiper and protected from the rain.

My eyes are hot and stinging as I stare at the only readable sentence.

This is why it has to be the end. Of everything. Be free, Whit. Six

"No," I choke out, my stomach tightening with shock. Sadness drenches me harder than the rain, and I sit in my car—alone, drenched, and utterly devasted. I let myself weep.

I take a few deep breaths and read the words again. Suddenly, sadness turns to anger, and a ripple of rage surges through me as I crumple the wet note and drop it onto the car floor.

"That *asshole*!" I grunt through gritted teeth.

I knew he couldn't do it. I knew he wasn't capable of feeling something real and lasting and beyond just the instant gratification of a one-night stand.

"He hasn't changed," I whisper through more tears. "He'll never change."

The moment he realized we were more than friends and more than sex, he ran. He fucking *ran*.

I slam my palm into the steering wheel, thinking how much of a freaking *idiot* I am for thinking that he could be something more.

But I knew all along. A living, breathing heartbreak.

thirty-two

Whitney

"No. Nope. Absolutely freaking not!" Melody flails her skinny arms around in disgust, pacing through the kitchen as I force some coffee down my throat.

"I told you everything, Mel. He had a change of heart." I swallow a gulp of coffee and fight the urge to cry for the hundredth time in the last twelve hours.

She grabs her neon hair and shakes her head vigorously. "I'm just not buying it. He told you he had feelings for you, seemed totally head over heels, and then he left you a note out of the blue saying it's over? *Everything*? Even your lifelong friendship?"

"Yes," I blurt, my voice cracking unexpectedly. "That's what happened. Are you really surprised?" I set my mug in the sink and lean against the counter, feeling like my whole body is too heavy and weak to stay standing. "We always knew he was an asshole. He got a little too close to something real, something beyond *sex*, with someone he actually gave a damn about, and he ran as far and fast as he possibly could."

Melody purses her lips and gently touches my arm,

and I feel bad for snapping at her. "Not *that* much of an asshole," she says. "Not enough of an asshole to throw away twenty-eight years of inseparable friendship." She knits her brows together. "Are you sure that's all the note said?"

I puff out a breath. "Whatever else it said got ruined by the rain. But I saw what I needed to see. I saw that his mind is made up."

"He wouldn't just *do* that. He loves you. You saw it in his eyes."

I pull in a shaky breath and hold my palm to my forehead. "I did. And I got up and left my date with Peter because I realized that Chase is the one. Or at least I thought he was. I thought I was going to drive to him, and we were going to have some magical, movie moment where we kiss and hug and admit that we've loved each other all along."

"Wait a second… He doesn't know you feel this way?" she asks slowly, staring over her cup of coffee, the wheels in her vibrant, pink brain turning way too fast.

"No," I whisper, another wave of regret and sadness washing over me. "I left his place to go get ready for my date with Peter, and that's the last time we talked. I didn't realize…" I shut my eyes and fight the need to sob. "I didn't know how I really felt until it was too late."

Melody jumps like she's about to burst right out of her skin. "Well, you have to tell him! Are you insane?"

"I'm not telling him anything." I tie my hair up into a ponytail and glance at the clock on the oven. I have to leave for the hospital in ten minutes, and I've never wanted to go to work less in my life. "He made his choice."

I walk toward the to door to get my bag off the hook, and Melody leaps in front of me, grabbing my shoulders with both hands. "He doesn't have all the information!" she squeals, shaking me.

"Mel, I love you to death. And your enthusiasm in inspiring. But you know what they say about tigers and how they can't change their stripes?"

"Yeah…"

"Well, they say the same thing about sinfully hot quarterbacks." I swing my bag over my arm. "Chase just remembered who he is. Who he'll always be. And now I've lost him forever, even as a friend." I bite my lip and swallow hard. "I think that's the worst part."

"Cuz, no! You can't just give up!"

"I'm not giving up, Mel. I was ready. I was ready to dive headfirst into the craziest, riskiest relationship imaginable. He's the one who gave it up."

She cups my cheeks with both hands and smushes my face. "Before he knew how you really feel!" she exclaims.

"I don't think it matters how I feel. The proof is literally written on a piece of notebook paper. He's done. He's out. It was too much, too deep, too…real. Chase Kennedy doesn't do *real*, and that was just his characteristically jackass way of reminding me."

"Cuzzie…" Melody gives me a soft hug, rubbing my back lovingly. "I'm so sorry. I saw the sparkle in your eyes that he brought. He's always brought it, but especially recently. I'm so, so sorry."

I let a tear slide down my face as I pull back and force a smile for Mel. "I'll be all right."

Eventually. I hope.

I walk out of the townhouse and get into my car, realizing that I've literally never lived without Chase before. I've never gone a single day on this earth where he wasn't a part of my life.

I pull out of the parking lot, and the morning sun beats down through my windshield. I can't hate Chase Kennedy. It's not physically possible. All I can do is miss him.

And, God, do I miss him.

of that stiff-ass dickbag kissing Whitney's gorgeous hand a thousand times.

I tighten my jaw and bite down on my mouth guard as we jog toward the locker room, forcing myself to remember the way she smiled. She threw her head back and laughed. She chose him, and I did the right thing by stepping aside and not putting any confusing pressure on her.

I hope she doesn't hate me. I hope she read every word of that note and can fully understand why I had to let her go. I couldn't be such a selfish, entitled prick to stand in the way of the guy she truly wants.

My cleats dig into the mud, and I yank my helmet off while we walk through the tunnel. Fuck this feeling.

"You good, bro?" Dylan jogs up next to me, elbowing my side. "You do know we won, right?"

I nod, keeping my eyes fixed on the ground. "Yeah. I know."

"So what's with the…" He gestures vaguely at my obviously defeated demeanor.

"Remember the whole Whitney thing?" I say quietly.

"Yeah…you were gonna bang again and see how you felt about it. What's good with all that?"

I pinch the bridge of my nose. "It's over. It just…" I take a deep breath as we walk into the locker room. "Didn't work."

"Shit, dude."

"You were right about something, though," I say without thinking. "Everyone has a one. The one."

"Is she the one for you?" He's practically whispering as we sit on benches in the locker room, the other guys too distracted from the win to notice us.

"Yeah. Only problem is, I'm not the one for her. You failed to mention that that shit doesn't always go both ways."

"Kennedy…it's not—" He shakes his head.

"Whatever." I stand and open my locker. "I'm done thinking about it."

That's a lie.

Dylan holds his hands up and backs away. "Fair enough. Nice work on the field today."

I laugh sarcastically. I was total shit on the field today, regardless of what the scoreboard says.

I check my phone like a desperate teenager. Hoping for something from her. Anything. A text, a missed call, a fucking Snapchat. But nothing, of course.

I made my bed, and now I have to lie in it. Alone.

Just as I'm about to pull off my jersey, a stadium security officer walks into the locker room.

"Sorry about this everyone," he shouts over the noise, and the room grows quiet as we all notice him.

Coach Watson walks toward the front of the locker room. "What's going on?"

"There's a young woman out here…" He points toward the door. "Outside the locker room. She's demanding to speak with a player, and she says it's urgent."

Coach shakes his head and holds up a hand. "No, no media right now."

"She's not with the press or media," the security guy says. "She's asking for Chase Kennedy."

I jump, turning forward and rushing to the front of the room. My chest tightens, and a chill swirls down my spine at the thought that Whit might be out there.

My heart rate starts to pick up as I jog up to the officer. "Hey, yeah, I'll go talk with her. It's no big deal."

I glance behind me and meet Dylan's gaze. He gives me a nod and a cocky smile, and I know we're both thinking the same thing.

My head is buzzing as I walk into the corridor. The spot where I kissed her that day. The memory makes my heart flip.

"You listen, and you listen good!"

I turn around to find a tiny woman in flowery yoga pants with unmistakably pink hair speed-walking toward me.

"Melody," I say slowly, the disappointment of Whitney's absence settling in my gut.

She points a finger at me and presses it into my chest. "What the hell is the matter with you?"

I step back, so wishing I didn't have to explain this to Whitney's insane cousin right now. "Melody, look, what happened with us is really complicated. I'm not what Whitney needs or deserves. She told me herself I'm a living, breathing heartbreak." I swallow and look away, flashes of the kiss in the corridor slamming into my head.

"You are such an idiot!" She throws her hands in the air.

"Listen, you want to know the truth?" I run a hand through my sweaty hair and narrow my eyes at Melody. "I went to the restaurant the night of her date to tell her I love her. To tell her she's the one and we need to be together. But then I saw her. I saw her with…him. She was happy. He was kissing her hand like some sort of royal prince. I realized that I'm just a messy, cocky playboy, and getting in the way of her future with Mr. Perfect would be unfair."

Her jaw practically hits the floor, and she starts bouncing on her toes. "Oh my God," she says quickly.

"Why are you bouncing? Stop bouncing."

Now she's just full-on jumping. "You think she *liked* that guy?"

"I saw her, Melody. He's, like, her dream husband."

She can barely contain her smile now, which is giving me a tiny glimmer of hope and excitement. "But you're wrong! You're so totally stinking *wrong*. She was faking it. She said the hand-kiss grossed her out. She left the date to go find you! Whit ditched the pretentious bush fund guy—"

"Hedge fund," I interject with a soft laugh.

"Whatever. She left, and that's when she found your cowardly note!"

"Okay, ouch." My heart starts beating fast again. Now I feel like bouncing. "But if she read the note and wasn't actually into the Peter guy, why didn't she just call me and tell me that and clear everything up? I made it obvious in the note that I thought she wanted him, and I was getting out of the picture so she could have him."

"The note got destroyed in the rain. She could only read the very last part. She thought you—"

"Oh *shit*," I say slowly as every piece of this screwed-up puzzle starts coming together in my mind. "She thinks I dumped her."

The thought of Whitney assuming I got cold feet and ended things to go back to being a fuckboy twists a knife in my heart. She must have been so hurt. The image wrecks me.

Melody smacks my shoulder pads with both hands. "I *knew* you weren't a total asshole! I knew you two were meant to be."

I smile, then laugh, holding a hand to my head as the possibility of getting her back starts to become very, very real.

"Melody." I grab her shoulders and hold her gaze as firmly as possible in an attempt to steady both of us. "We have to get to the hospital."

She squeals and claps her hands excitedly. "Can we take the Lambo?"

I roll my eyes as we start rushing toward the garage. "Duh. I'm not going to profess my love for Whitney after rolling up in a VW Bug, or whatever you drive."

She smacks my side as our pace speeds up, and the buzz in the air becomes palpable. "Screw you. It's a Mini Cooper."

thirty-four

Whitney

I'm not even halfway through this shift, but it feels like I've been working for twenty hours. My head hurts, my heart aches, and every second I'm alone, I have to will myself not to cry.

I shuffle down the hallway to grab a vitals machine for a new patient, my feet feeling like they're sticking to the floor. "This," I mumble under my breath through gritted teeth. "This is why you were never supposed to fall for Chase freaking Kennedy. This is why you refused to ever get caught up in his magical spell."

The emergency room has been uncharacteristically empty today. Normally, I would be thankful for the lack of stress, but today I need to be more immersed in work than ever, just to keep from melting into a puddle on the linoleum.

"How we doing in here? Any improvement?" I roll the standing monitor into room sixteen and force a smile for a little boy who fell off his skateboard and ended up with eight stitches in his chin.

His mom squeezes his hand and beams at me. "We're hanging in there. Daddy's on his way."

I swallow the twist in my gut that screams with the desire for love and a family of my own. "I'm glad to hear that. You're gonna be just fine, Zachary."

Shaken up from his first ER visit, Zach looks at me with wide eyes and a toothy grin as I wrap the blood pressure cuff around his tiny arm. "You're pretty."

I relish the first bubble of genuine laughter that rises in my chest since the moment I read that stupid, wet note. "Thanks, Zach." I hold the thermometer in front of his mouth. "Now open wide."

Just as the thermometer starts beeping with a temperature read, Sky rushes into the room, the nursing assistant's shiny blond ponytail swinging behind her. "Whitney, there's something going on in the waiting room." Her bright eyes and giddy smile tell me that it's not something serious or medical.

I furrow my brow suspiciously. "Is everyone okay?"

"Yeah! I can take over in here, if you wanna go…" She glances back down the hallway. "Handle it."

"Okay," I say slowly, handing her the vitals machine and my clipboard with Zachary's records. "His vitals are normal. I'm requesting discharge papers and a prescription cream to help heal his stitches."

She nods quickly, still smiling. "Got it. Now please go!"

"All right, all right." I raise my hands and walk out of the room, wondering what bizarre thing could be happening—and potentially making this craptastic day even worse.

I head down the hallway, noticing a buzz of commotion rippling through the air. It doesn't seem urgent or bad, like a serious emergency. Everyone who walks past me looks happy and giddy, like Sky did.

I take a deep breath, wondering if I could possibly actually be losing my mind, and swing open the double doors that lead to the waiting room.

My heart somersaults, and chills race through my body as my brain starts to register what is happening in front of me.

"I have to see Whitney Cooper, now. She's a nurse here, and I know she's working, and… I just *have* to see her." Chase is leaning against the registration desk, his hair sweaty and his face smudged with dirt. He's wearing his pads and jersey, looking as if he literally just ran right off the field.

I try to make a sound, but nothing comes out.

Sandra, our front-desk assistant, is clicking a pen with her thumb. "I don't care who you are, young man. If there is no medical emergency, you can't enter the emergency room. Period!"

He runs his hands through his hair, still unaware of me standing in the corner by the doorway.

My stomach is flooded with butterflies now, and I can't decide whether I want to laugh or cry.

Sandra purses her lips. "Tell you what, son. When that sweet, handsome Elliot Danes came in here, he gave me a signed football for my son."

Chase claps his hands together and smiles. "I can sign a football!"

She shakes her head slowly. "How 'bout the jersey?"

He frowns with a laugh, looking down. "It's kind of dirty…"

Sandra glares at him. "My son would kill for a Chase Kennedy jersey. The quarterback." She waves a hand dramatically. "You wanna see our Whitney or not?"

Without another moment of hesitation, Chase pulls his jersey off right in the ER waiting room, eliciting some snickers and "ooohs" from the onlooking staff.

I hold a hand to my mouth and laugh softly as shirtless Chase rushes toward the door, stopping dead in his tracks when his eyes meet mine. "Whit…"

Every fiber of my body is begging me to jump into his arms—his sexy, loving, rock-hard arms—and melt into him and let him hold me forever.

"Chase, no," I croak, remembering the note, and the hurt, and refusing to let myself give in to him.

By now, on this very slow day in the emergency room, there's a decent-sized audience watching our exchange. Nurses and technicians and even a doctor or two have gathered in the waiting room to watch a dirty and shirtless NFL quarterback chase after me.

"Whitney…" He places his hands on my shoulders, making my knees turn to water. "I messed up. I thought I was doing the right thing, and—"

With all the strength I have, I pull his arms off me and wiggle out of his embrace. "You made up your mind. You said it pretty clearly in your letter. You said it was the end of everything between us."

"I know, but you have to just listen to me."

"Chase, stop." I'm fighting tears now. "That note broke my heart. I left the date to go find you. To tell you that I—"

"That she loves you!" Suddenly, Melody is bursting through the door with a wild grin and frantic arms.

"What part of 'wait in the car' did you not understand?" Chase asks her.

She rushes to us, panting breathlessly. "I know, I know. But listen, Whit, he was trying to be all heroic and let you fly free." She makes a bird motion with her hands. "He thought you wanted Peter, and—"

"Wait, who's Peter, now?" Sandra chimes in from the front desk.

"Can I please do the talking?" Chase begs.

"Wait, why did you think I wanted to be with him? He completely sucked. He made me realize just how much I want…someone else." I meet Chase's gaze, and the fire between us burns at a thousand degrees.

His lips part at my words, and he takes in a slow breath. "I went to the restaurant to tell you how I feel. But then I saw you through the window, and—"

"Um, creepy?" a nurse blurts out.

Chase throws her a look and then refocuses on me. "And you looked so happy. And he seemed like the textbook, cookie-cutter Mr. Husband, and I felt like I would just get in your way. Because that's what you want. And all this was explained in my note, but…"

"The rain," I whisper, feeling a smile playing at my mouth as the world floats and swims around me. "I was just faking it on that awful date. I was trying to give it a chance. What did you want to say? At the restaurant?"

He steps back, his chest rising and falling. "Nit Whit, I'm in love with you. And I used to be scared to say that, but now it's, like, my favorite phrase," he says through a laugh. "And I'm starting to think I have been for a really, really long time." He swallows and reaches for my face, stroking my cheek with his thumb and inching closer to me. "It took a long and twisted road to get here, but you were there for every turn. I know I'm not a perfect, picket-fence kinda guy, and I sure as hell don't match the definition of boyfriend material in the dictionary, but…" He holds me close now, our lips inches apart. "You're the love of my damn life, Whit."

I choke on a laugh as a tear rolls down my cheek.

Chase wipes it away. "Please be with me. As my best friend. And so, so much more. You're it. You're the one."

More happy tears fall down my face as I realize that my heart is squeezing and flipping, and some aching, lonely part of myself has just suddenly become complete. Probably the part that's loved Chase for more than twenty years. Everything in me right now trusts him, adores him, and needs him. "That note was so sad. I thought you changed your mind, like you wanted to go back to being—"

"No." He fixes his gaze on mine with certainty. "Hell no. I thought I was doing what's best for you, but goddammit, I'm what's best for you, Whitney."

"You've always been the one, Six."

I stand on my toes and press my lips to his, both of us laughing into the kiss. Through the muffled buzz in my head, I hear the hospital staff cheering and hooting.

Warmth courses through me, and I let myself lean into his hands. Those hands that have wiped my tears since I was four. Those hands that throw game-winning passes in the NFL. Those hands that I'm going to hold forever.

"You don't think I'm a living, breathing heartbreak anymore, right?" he whispers, pressing his forehead against mine.

"No, Chase. You're living, breathing magic."

epilogue

Whitney

"You know how I used to be the king of the single life?" Chase bites his lip and nods as he laces his fingers through mine while we walk into the stadium elevator.

I groan and roll my eyes. "Yes. I remember."

"Well, now I'm king of the relationship life. I have the best girlfriend and the best relationship. I'm winning even bigger now." He kisses my forehead as the elevator shoots us up to the private party room for the annual South Florida Riders VIP Christmas party.

The box rooms and suites throughout the stadium are decorated with garlands and lights and all manner of football-related ornaments.

Chase is radiating charm, and every time our eyes meet, he seems to adore me more. We're running a little late because as soon as he saw me in my little red dress and tights, we just *had* to have sex.

Oops.

"If it isn't Quarterback and Miss Quarterback!" A noticeably round and glowing Frankie hugs us both as her tall, handsome husband gives Chase a pat on the shoulder.

Leo drags Chase off to go get a drink, and I peek at my phone, wondering where Melody is. I snagged her an extra ticket to come to the party tonight, and she promised she'd meet me here.

"Hi!" Asher scampers up to me and wraps his arms around my leg.

"Well, hello." I grin, looking at Jessica, and she beams with pride.

"He's really come out of his shell." She ruffles his hair. "Just wants to be everybody's friend now, don't you, bud?"

Asher looks up at her and nods eagerly, racing away to go find Elliot.

"He's amazing," I say, giving Jessica a warm hug.

"He's tied for the love of my life." She shrugs and sips a drink. "My heart is totally owned by the two of them."

Elliot shoots us a smile and a wave.

I find Chase, and my heart flips and squeezes, still utterly in shock that he's *mine*. He's actually totally and completely mine. We've been an official couple for a few months now, and it's basically like being best friends on mega steroids.

I never knew happiness until I opened my heart to Chase, and I've fallen so deeply in love, I can barely see straight.

He catches my gaze, and his deep-brown eyes crackle with joy and admiration and some sweet, sexy, fiery love. He seems extra bubbly tonight, like he gets more excited and vibrant every moment.

I make my way over to him, accepting a cocktail

from a server with a tray, my gaze totally fixed on the man of my dreams.

He's talking to Matt McKenzie, who, though Chase will deny it to the grave, has become a new friend this season.

"This right here…" He wraps a rock-solid arm around my waist and pulls me close and tight against him. "This is what it's all about."

Matt smiles and shakes his head slowly. "You two were really in a literal baby group together? What a story."

I laugh and turn to my boyfriend, lost in the flawless cut of his jawline and the playful smile on his mouth. "It's true. Mommy and Me."

"She was always my best friend. And she was always the one. My dumb ass just took way too long to figure it out." He kisses my cheek, and my chest swarms with butterflies.

I don't think I'll ever get used to being loved by Chase. It gets more magical every day.

"Y'all are inspiring, that's for sure." Matt chuckles.

Chase places a firm hand on Matt's shoulder. "The torch is yours now, Junior. The fates of all single women in South Florida are in your hands. Don't let me down."

I give an exaggerated eye roll and stifle a laugh just as I turn to the door to see Melody bouncing in.

"You made it!" I rush over and give her a squeeze.

"Uh, duh! You think I'd give up a chance to see my favorite cousin? I've been practically dying of loneliness since you moved out to live with Chase."

I snort. "Mel, I only officially moved out a couple weeks ago."

"And my heart has yet to heal," she teases. "Although I can't lie. I'm so insanely happy for you. The glow is so, *so* real. You found your fated mate."

I narrow my eyes. "My fated mate? You are something else, cuz. Come on, I'll introduce you to everyone."

I drag Melody around and proudly show her off to all the Riders guys and their families.

"Who's that?" she whispers into my ear, nodding subtly at Dylan Rivera.

"Dylan. He's the kicker. He and Chase are super close. He's a pretty laidback, focused kinda guy."

Melody bites her lip and fixes her gaze on Dylan, who notices her and nods, looking intrigued and curious.

"Go say hi," I encourage her, feeling a burning and magnetic need to get back to Chase. I've really become one of those people.

I walk back to him, leaning against his shoulder and sipping my drink, letting a smile pull at my lips as he tells some exaggerated story about the national championship when we were in college.

I drown out the noise and let myself float in the suspended joy of this moment, of this man, of the feeling that I've spent my whole life searching for, having no idea it was always right in front of me.

"Give us a second. We'll be right back." Chase slips his hand into mine and pulls me away from the crowd.

I giggle and hold my hand to my mouth, buzzing with the constant magic of Chase. "Where are we going?" I lean into his ear as we rush out of the room. "There is no way you want to bang again *already*."

He raises his brows and gives me a cocky smile. "I mean, I'm down if you are. But that's not my plan, you little wild thing."

I squeeze his hand, and he takes me into the elevator, hitting the button for the ground floor and kissing me passionately as we glide down.

His hands are holding my waist tight, and his eyes are even more sparkly than usual. His smile is reckless and expressive.

"What on earth are we doing, Six?" I say through a laugh.

Chase presses a finger to my lips. "Just follow me."

The doors slide open, and we walk out into the stadium corridor. There's no one around, and my heels click on the concrete as I grip Chase's hand and hurry to keep up with him.

Suddenly, we turn a corner, and we're in the tunnel, looking out onto the field. It's completely dark, and there's not a soul in sight.

"Oh, I get it," I say quietly. "You wanna have sex on the field."

"Once again, wild child, I would be down. But that's not actually why we're here." He nods toward the dark field and tightens his grip on my fingers. "Come with me."

As we step onto the grass, I look around at the stands. The stadium is enormous and overwhelming, and I'm pretty amazed that this place can feel some comfortable for Chase when it's filled with people.

The air is slightly chilly, a typical South Florida December night, and he is still dragging me out to the middle of the field.

I laugh and follow him, until we finally reach the fifty-yard line.

He stops and fixes his gaze on mine, holding both of my hands and looking at me like I'm the most precious and beautiful and treasured thing Chase Kennedy has ever seen.

Suddenly, a low boom sounds all over the field, and every blaring light comes on at once. The field lights up, and a white glow pours over us. Passion and love and the deepest of friendship mixes and explodes between us, and my knees feel weak just looking at him. Still.

"Nit Whit," he says slowly, squeezing both my hands, his lips inches from mine.

"Six…" I smile, looking around and feeling a swirl of excitement racing down my spine.

"You're the most perfect, hilarious, and brilliant woman I've ever met. I never knew how lost I was, how empty I was, until I fell for you. I may have taught you sex," he says softly through a charming laugh, "but you taught me love. I've had the absolute honor of being your best friend for twenty-eight years. And tonight, I want to ask you…"

He drops to one knee, and my heart flips a hundred times. I can barely breathe as I feel a tear of joy start to fall from my eye.

"If you'll be my best friend forever?"

I let out something between a laugh and a happy sob and nod as fast as my head can manage. "Yes. Oh my God, yes!"

He opens a box containing a glittery diamond and slides it onto my shaking finger. He stands up and kisses me, lifting me off the ground.

I laugh and hold him tighter than I've ever held anything, looking around at the stadium and feeling like the luckiest girl on the planet.

"I'm so glad you said yes," he says through an emotional laugh, "because…"

He looks at the giant Jumbotron on the side of the stadium, and it lights up in blaring aqua and white—Riders colors—with the words *SHE SAID YES!* shining and flashing.

"You're freaking kidding me, Six!" I melt into him and let the purest joy I've ever felt wash over me like a tidal wave.

"Now I'm gonna be the king of married life!" he says excitedly.

"You can't do anything small, can you?" I wipe a tear of happiness from my cheek and admire the moment.

Then everyone comes running out onto the field, hollering and cheering. Elliot pops a bottle of champagne, and Asher jumps up and down.

"You did it, man!" Leo throws his arm around Chase's shoulders. "Now…there isn't anyone but Whitney."

Chase smiles at me and shakes his head, beaming with love. "There never really was."

The Ride Isn't Over!

Fall in love with Dylan and Melody when these total opposites can't help but attract.

SOUTH FLORIDA RIDERS · BOOK FOUR

Want to know the day Breezie Bennett releases a new book?

Sign up for The Cool Breeze and stay updated on all things Breezie at https://breeziebennett.com/.

about the author

Breezie Bennett has had her fingers on a keyboard since she was a middle schooler writing sports romances about her brother's baseball team. A graduate of the University of Florida, she is fluent in Mandarin Chinese, can dance on pointe, and has been known to shotgun a beer in 5.2 seconds. When not writing romance, you'll find her on a Florida beach with her two dogs, Ginger and Rosemary, and a playlist full of Pink Floyd and Lil Wayne.

Made in United States
North Haven, CT
18 February 2022